Weekend with Avery

Tammy Godfrey

Phoenix Voices Publishing

Copyright © 2023 by Tammy Godfrey

All rights reserved. No part of this publication may be reproduced, stored or transmitted in any form or by any means, electronic, mechanical, photocopying, recording, scanning, or otherwise without written permission from the publisher. It is illegal to copy this book, post it to a website, or distribute it by any other means without permission.

This novel is entirely a work of fiction. The names, characters and incidents portrayed in it are the work of the author's imagination. Any resemblance to actual persons, living or dead, events or localities is entirely coincidental.

Tammy Godfrey asserts the moral right to be identified as the author of this work.

Tammy Godfrey has no responsibility for the persistence or accuracy of

URLs for external or third-party Internet Websites referred to in this publication and does not guarantee that any content on such Websites is, or will remain, accurate or appropriate.

Designations used by companies to distinguish their products are often claimed as trademarks. All brand names and product names used in this book and on its cover are trade names, service marks, trademarks and registered trademarks of their respective owners. The publishers and the book are not associated with any product or vendor mentioned in this book. None of the companies referenced within the book have endorsed the book.

Contents

1. Chapter One — 1
2. Chapter Two — 7
3. Chapter Three — 15
4. Chapter Four — 22
5. Chapter Five — 29
6. Chapter Six — 34
7. Chapter Seven — 42
8. Chapter Eight — 50
9. Chapter Nine — 60
10. Chapter Ten — 74
11. Chapter Eleven — 81
12. Chapter Twelve — 88

13.	Chapter Thirteen	95
14.	Chapter Fourteen	104
15.	Chapter Fifteen	105
16.	Chapter Sixteen	112
Except from Christmas With Avery		116
About the Author		118
Also by Tammy Godfrey		119

Chapter One

I knew my morning coffee was going to get me into trouble. I'd had the same thing every workday morning for two months: a medium-light blended Vanilla decaf latte. It cost three dollars and forty-five cents, including tax. Having them three to five times a day, I knew I spent over ninety dollars a month on this indulgence; I had this addiction that needed feeding. I was in a sorry state and starting to think about a twelve-step program. My name's Avery, and I'm addicted to lattes.

I knew someone else that had an addiction to some Starbucks concoction too. I didn't know his name, but he's hot in a California-beach-guy-in-a-suit way. One morning in late May, things changed.

I'd just gotten my morning "fix" the irresistible latte and started to push my way out of the crowded coffee shop salivating over the odor of the brew as it wafted to my nostrils. Then "he" appeared my handsome mystery man, on his way to get his morning concoction and squarely in front of me.

"Oh, hello," he said. We both stopped and faced each other in the narrow foyer of the shop. We both smiled. He had nice teeth.

I looked up into his steel-grey eyes and at his sun-kissed locks.

"Hello," I said, "Are you here for your morning injection too?"

"Of course," he said. "I see you almost every day. I'm Benjamin Elliot or Ben, my friends call me, or my mom calls me Elliot Case."

"Elliot Case, why?" I asked, really wanting to know.

"No, Benjamin Elliot Case, my mom calls me Elliot. She wanted to name me that, and my Dad said I had to be named after my Grandfather," Ben started. "I can't believe I just told you that."

"I'm Avery," I held my coffee into my left hand with my large purse and put my right hand out to shake his hand. I thought how clever I'd been to remember not to give my last name to a stranger. "Nice to meet you officially after all these months of passing each other."

Impulsively he asked, "Will you wait for me? Do you have time, or are you late for work?" Those steel-grey eyes looked at me, and I suddenly felt like a soft ice cream sandwich on a hot summer day. I got all warm and mushy inside.

"Yeah, I have time," I said slowly, "I'll be outside." We squeezed past each other, and I went through the outer door onto the sidewalk.

I wondered why I was suddenly so willing to meet a strange man, although a good-looking one. I still suffered from the sudden exit nine months earlier of the last man in my life, and I certainly was not looking for another jolt of pain right now.

A hundred feet to my right, there was an empty park bench.

I angled towards it, deposited my large bag, and then sat to see the door to the coffee shop. I felt awkward sitting as the world whirled by me all on their way to some meaningful employment.

I also thought I should do this more often.

I took the first luscious sip of my morning latte. I sighed with what was the closest thing to an orgasm that I'd had in almost a year that I didn't give myself. Happens with every cup. It's the only orgasmic rush I've had in a very long time.

I quickly tried to assess how I looked. I puffed up my hair a little, not something I would typically do and hard to do with the specifical curtain hair around the face, but I have long bangs style I wore. The only reason I know the type is because I've had many friends tell me that I look like the girl on *Fifty Shade Of Grey*. I popped open my purse, pulled my compact out, and did a little brush up to my makeup. I didn't meet a guy this good looking regularly; he'd certainly turned my head.

Ten minutes later, I turned towards *Starbucks*, and Ben appeared, looking around for me. I waved wildly until he saw me. He strolled towards me, and I got a chance to look at him more carefully: early-thirties or late twenties, tasseled loafers, no sox, snug jeans that showed off long, athletic legs and made me wonder about what else they might hide, a white dress shirt with the sleeves rolled up two turns, and aviator sunglasses pushed upon his head. Best of all, though, was his smile. Ben had the perfect smile with teeth that made some orthodontist proud and his parents poor, no doubt.

"I almost feel as though I know you," Ben said as he arrived at the bench. I gestured beside me, and he sat. "I've seen you here almost every day for months. I even notice what you wear; it's become a contest for me to see if I can remember when you last wore the same thing. For instance, today's blazer was last Wednesday. Right?" He'd gestured at my jacket as he talked.

I laughed, "Right, probably. I don't remember." I paused and looked at him as he savored the first sip from his Starbucks cup.

I watched his eyes roll up into his head as that magnificent first sip touched his palette. "What do you drink?"

"This week, it's a cinnamon-dusted latte light brew coffee. I change from time to time; must be daring and take risks." He looked at me and sniffed the air; "You're having a Vanilla latte. I did that two weeks ago. Yummy," He paused and added, "I also like the hint of perfume you're wearing, Romance Rose?" I laughed and nodded at his acute sense of smell.

We sat and talked on the busy street as we savored our coffees. I shared that I ran the art department for a medium-sized ad agency a block to the south. He'd heard of the company.

Ben talked about his work managing the investment portfolio for a charitable foundation a block to the north. I got the sense that he'd married his job. He did mention having grown up near Seattle as well as still having family out there.

He mentioned he'd been an eagle scout growing up and was skilled at mountaineering and loved to camp out. However, he hadn't done anything with those hobbies since he'd gotten his MBA a few years earlier.

This guy appeared to be all work and no play. I guess I'd become that way too. I knew I was hiding in my career to escape the whole relationship and bar scene.

Why now did my head suddenly think that dating this relative stranger would be a good idea? I could hear the voices. My rational voice intervened and told me to stop having such dangerous ideas.

During our chat, we somehow signaled that we were both 'unattached' and then kept talking about a hundred other things in that 'get to know you' conversation.

Somehow, I shared that I'd grown up outside of Durham, New Hampshire, the daughter of a college professor at the state university. We established that I was five years, four months, and four days younger than he was.

Ben impressed me with his effortless style and polite demeanor. He smiled often, and I found myself drawn deeper and deeper into those beautiful eyes.

I even confess to flirting slightly. Maybe I was ready to venture forth into the world of dating again. All my friends seemed to have a foot planted squarely against my rear end, pushing me to come back on the circuit. I'd turned down uncounted blind dates.

Our cups slowly emptied, and I know I prolonged taking the last sip of my drink. As we talked and got to know each other. I sat and spun the cardboard protectors around our nearly empty cups, each of us slightly nervous and reticent before the other in this odd mating dance.

I didn't want to break the spell that seemed to have captured both of us. An aura of comfortable friendship that hinted at a potential for something more had descended upon us. I felt it and figured he did too.

Eventually, an hour after we sat down, Ben's cell phone beeped and vibrated quietly at his side. He jumped and, after looking at the source of the call, routed the call to voicemail. "I should be going," he said reluctantly. "I can't say when I've enjoyed my coffee more. Will you meet me here at about the same time tomorrow? I think the weather is supposed to be good."

There was that inviting smile again.

I nodded enthusiastically and agreed to our informal date.

We rose, shook hands, simultaneously said, "Until tomorrow," and headed in our respective directions to work. I had a smile on my face for a change, and I bet Ben did too.

I found it hard to concentrate at work because of Ben. He'd been so engaging and cordial. I'd left my last relationship with a low self-image, mostly created by my then live-in boyfriend, who had frequently told me how worthless I was. Even now, many months later, I struggled to overcome the psychological luggage from that four-year relationship.

At one point, when I was in the women's restroom at work, I stopped and looked at myself in the large mirror. Today was my black and red day. I had black shoes, black tights, a black skirt, and a black blazer with a blazing red scoop neck top. My dark brown hair only added to the message of invisibility I was trying to send.

I stood profile to the mirror. I still needed to lose twenty pounds. The blazer hid that ten of those pounds were becoming a paunch and the other ten excess luggage in my butt. That said, my figure could be described as a full rack. I hadn't started to sag. I blame my breast on my Grandma's genes, and my mom said it was not fair. She was small and had work done. I still turned heads when I wore the right, snug-fitting top or bent over wearing something loose. I could be a surprisingly good tease when I wanted to be. I have worn sports bras and other tight-fitting bras, so my shirts I want because I will fit always had to go up one size.

Based on what others told me, I was pretty. I had a 'girl next door' kind of face, smooth and oval without many fashion models' angular cheekbones or jaws. Blue eyes and bright white teeth accented the Mediterranean complexion I'd inherited from my father, a man of Spanish heritage.

I sighed and went back to work while rethinking how I could fit in more exercise and less food into my regime.

Chapter Two

Tuesday morning, I picked up my usual latte, and as I left the store, Ben arrived. I just said, "Bench," as we passed each other and gestured towards where we'd sat the day before. We gave each other big smiles. What an excellent way to start the morning, I thought.

This man was gorgeous. I'd had several Ben fantasies throughout the previous night, including one resulting in a self-inflicted orgasm of charming proportions. I shivered as I remembered the wave of pleasure. God bless batteryoperated toys. I hadn't had to bring them out for months. This guy did things to me.

By sunrise, however, I'd decided I'd seen Ben through rosecolored glasses and that he couldn't be 'that' sound. My fantasies were over the top. No guy could do what I was thinking in my head. Nope, not going to happen. Yet here he was again in his tall and handsome splendor. My heart did a little flip-flop as I walked to the bench with my daily coffee.

I resolved to find out Ben's three hundred bad habits, so I could get grounded again. I developed this puppy-love crush. I seemed to grow overnight, heavily weighted by personality traits assigned by my own imagination.

A few minutes later, he joined me on the same bench with his coffee de jour. He told me he often came by bus from his condo. I confessed to a studio apartment and proudly told him I usually walked the short distance unless the weather was unbearable when I'd call a taxi. I noted that his neighborhood was in Lake Washington. It was considerably more upscale than my modest apartment, even though I had a place on South Hudson Street.

I asked him some more about his work as an investment manager at the Foundation. That started a discussion about risk-taking and being a risk-taker. I confessed to not knowing where I stood on the risk-taking since I'd grown up pretty sheltered life until college life. I have been in only two long-term relationships. On the other hand, while in those relationships, some exciting and daring things had happened.

Ben asked about my last relationship, even if carefully. I volunteered the relationship's disastrous nature and how it had dragged me down for the last couple of years.

Predictably he asked how it had dragged me down. After a few months of wooing me and getting me to move in with him, I explained that Bill had become a bastard. I'd become the slave and stayed way too long, expecting that the situation would change. We'd talk, and Bill would change for a few days or a week but slip back into his demanding and demeaning ways. He liked running me down. I lost the ability to resist as my self-esteem disappeared until finally, one day, I woke up from a bad dream and just walked out. I admitted my co-dependence in the situation. I probably went into too much detail, but it was cathartic, and Ben seemed to be actively listening as I dumped.

Finally, I ran out of steam, thinking to get it all out so he can leave me before I get any more into him.

Ben reached over and touched my arm gently, looked straight into my eyes, and said, "Avery, I'm not Bill."

His statement surprised me on several different levels. For one, it hinted that Ben wanted some kind of relationship. Based on what I'd been saying, it also implied that he would be someone that would push me upward rather than pull me downward. It also suggested he wouldn't allow me to slip away in some negative co-dependent state.

I wondered if I was reading too much into his looks and his comments. No, he wasn't leaving.

Ben suddenly said, "Avery, I know you've only known me for two of the past twenty-six hours, but I have a question to ask you — a proposition."

All I could think was the other shoe was about to drop.

He looked encouragingly at me, waiting for me to invite his question. My curiosity was piqued, and so I nodded while displaying one of my genuine happy smiles. I figured he would ask for a date on the weekend.

He went on, "Would you spend the weekend with me in Aspen, Colorado?"

I know my mouth flopped open. I could feel the chilly morning air rushing in as I inhaled.

Ben babbled on, "It wouldn't cost you anything. I'll pay for everything. You'd be doing me a huge favor. I'll pay for everything, including whatever outfits you figure you'll need for the trip and the event I have to be at, and you can keep those like your own. Oh, and I assure you I am of good moral character, have no designs on your body, and ... well, would you be willing to fly out there with me? I think it might be interesting for you if not a little bit of fun. I just really, really need a "temporary girlfriend'."

Was I just going into the real-life *Fifty Shades Of Grey*? I have to admit I like books and movies when others didn't, but I didn't want to be in a real-life one. Somehow my mind flitted to the love scene of the books. I'd remembered my last midnight orgasm with fondness that washed over me after envisioning and the room of red. I tried to push that out of my head as not a relevant decision-making factor. The scene reappeared anyway.

The brief discussion we'd had about risk-taking and getting away from one's comfort zone to grow also flew through my brain, nothing wrong with my short-term memory.

I had never done anything spontaneous before in my life, and now I had the chance to do it. I think I shut my mouth about then. I thought for a split second, then blurted out, "Yes, I'd love to," before my rational self could intervene. I added, "Tell me more."

"Great," he said. "There's a wedding out there, and while I'm not "in" it, I'm sort of an important guest. A lot of my old friends will be there, as well as my entire family."

"You need a 'temporary girlfriend or a date?" I posited.

Ben replied tentatively, "Actually, I need more than a date if you're willing to rescue me from my solitary loner existence. My brother, sisters, and best friends have all given me increasing grief for years about not having a girlfriend" He paused.

"Yes, I know what that feels like," I said slowly, my brain actively engaged in assessing this new situation. Little red flags were waving as I wondered why Ben hadn't dated and described himself as a solitary loner. What's wrong with him?

He went on, "So I told a little lie when I was back there for a couple of days over Christmas."

"You told them you had a steady girlfriend," I said flatly.

Ben nodded.

"I am the only hope you have to rescue your sorry ass and reputation from friends and family," I smiled widely as I tortured him.

"Yes," he said sheepishly. He looked down.

"Why are you in this situation?" I asked in a more severe tone, wondering if Ben was gay. Now I was turning the tables on him about the sorry state of our love lives. He became the confessor.

"Well," Ben said, looking up and talking with more great animation, "I work too hard. I started the Foundation I told you about. I spend just about all of my time on it. I haven't really had much of a social life since I got out of grad school. I tried a couple of times, but they wanted more than I could give, and I never told my family I was seeing anyone. Now it's just a few family events every now and then or an occasional friend stopping by Seattle from out of town."

"You 'started' the Foundation...charitable Foundation?" I asked incredulously. "You said you worked at one yesterday, but I didn't realize it was yours."

"Yeah," he said modestly. "The initial money that started it was part of a modest inheritance from my parents. They died in a plane crash about ten years ago."

I stammered out, "Oh, I'm so sorry."

"Thank you, and it's okay now," Ben said in a reverent tone. "It was a long time ago. They were on their way to Europe on a Swissair flight that crashed off the coast of Canada. I'd just started grad school for an MBA when it happened."

"Oh," I said, not knowing where to take the conversation.

I think Ben read my confusion as he studied my face. He took my hand in his, and I willingly squeezed back to show I appreciated his honesty and to show my sympathy.

"So anyway, about Colorado. The trip is to the wedding of my youngest sister," Ben said more energetically. "She's been engaged for the past two years to this guy I've met twice during the holiday seasons. The wedding is Saturday afternoon in Aspen five days from today."

He paused and checked in with me to see if I was still on his wavelength. I was. He went on, "We'll fly to Aspen from here, on Friday afternoon if you can do it. If you can spare an extra day on Monday, we can see if there's spring skiing. Otherwise, I'll have you back here late Sunday night. Your duties would be to act as a serious girlfriend, whatever that means. Are you good at acting?"

"I opt for the ski day," I said with a smile, "I think I can play-act my way through this. I'm not sure I like the idea of supporting your white lies to your family, but I guess I will help rescue you."

Inside me, a little voice was screaming, "No! No! No! Don't do it." I could also hear another little voice saying, "Finally!

About time! Get out there, date, and be social! This guy's cute." The two voices in my head were fighting with each other, not unusual these days.

Ben broke into a big grin. "Thank you so much. You are saving me from the torture at the hands of people that say they love me."

My rationale self-kick is, "Now, what kind of duties will I be expected to perform? I supposed to know you better than that you hang out at the Starbucks at seven-thirty most mornings trolling for a 'temporary girlfriend'?" using air quotes as I talked.

Ben thought for a few seconds, then said, "We have a few days before we would go. If you're free, we can keep meeting like this in the mornings, and how about Thursday? I take you out to dinner, and I'll show you my condo? You should see it before we go to Colorado? It's special, and all my brothers and sisters have seen the place at one time or another during stopovers in Seattle."

"I would be delighted," I replied with my smile. "This gets more complicated, but the whole idea excites me. I always did want to be in the theater. What's that quote? Something about 'all the world's a stage and all the men and women merely players.'"

Ben said, "I've got to go, but here's my business card. My home numbers on the back. It also has my e-mail on it."

"Oh, let me give you one of mine too," I said. I dug frantically in my shoulder bag until I found my cardholder and produced a card. I wrote my home number on the back: in for a penny, in for a pound.

As I wrote, I suddenly turned to Ben and asked, "You said the Foundation was the reason you don't have a girlfriend. There's another reason, right?"

Ben studied my face as he accepted my business card, "Yes," he said slowly, "I guess I'm scared of relationships. I haven't been in a serious relationship since I was in grad school. To tell the truth, that one sort of hurting me a lot when it fell apart. She had more ambitions about the corporate world than I did at the time."

He went on, "Further, I guess you should know, I have a weird philosophy about relationships now, and I'm guessing that no one in their right mind would probably want to get involved with me until I change somehow. I'll tell you one of these days. Lastly, I guess I'm scared of commitment; I've never found anyone that inspired me to use the three words every girl wants to hear."

I caught his eye and said, "Then don't." He looked puzzled, and so I added, "Just take one day at a time. You don't have to commit to anything other than being here right now with me." I added, "Okay, boyfriend'?"

He laughed and said, "Okay, 'girlfriend.'" We both got up to leave.

I then said, "Oh, you have homework. I'd like to know what you told them about your girlfriend when you were out there. I hope you didn't give them a name or tell them I was blond. What expectations will I have to meet?"

He laughed and said, "I'll make a list. Until tomorrow - and thank you, thank you, thank you so much. You don't know what this means to me. I'll be forever in your debt."

He leaned in and kissed me on the cheek. I squeezed his hand.

With that, he turned and strode away from me with a happy flair to his walk. I think my mouth was hanging open again.

My cheek still burned from his kiss.

Chapter Three

Each of the next three mornings, we spent an hour learning about each other. Ben also realized we'd have some time to talk on the plane ride to Aspen.

I brought a framework I found on the Internet about relationships to focus on particular parts of our lives besides our jobs. We spent Wednesday on genealogy and how we felt about our families, member by member. We also talked about our resumes, where we'd lived, our work, career paths, and what we sought by working.

Thursday, we talked about our religious upbringing that, for both of us, left us spiritual yet not churchy. We also talked about our exercise regimes and goals. We briefly talked about our hopes and aspirations for our lives and then our life goals, breaking off to go to work and expecting to meet for dinner.

Ben called me about one o'clock on Thursday and told me he'd booked dinner at Altura, one of the more upscale restaurants in Seattle and one that was far out of my league in terms of prices.

I'd never been there.

Given the restaurant's nature, I figured I'd better rethink my 'going out for a bite after work' mode of dress. What worked in the office would definitely not work at Altura. Thus, for a change, I left work at four o'clock, much to the surprise of my colleagues, went to the hairdressers and got the results, and then headed back to my studio to change.

Ben had said he'd pick me up about seven-thirty. I was ready about seven and pacing the floor, doing little adjustments to my look every other circuit. Nervous pacing in my studio is hard to do because it is so small. I had to circle the coffee table to get any steam up at a pace. I was nervous.

I'd decided to wear my LBD, my little black dress. I picked that for several reasons. First, it is probably the most fabulous and sexiest dress I have, the wavy hemline oscillating three to six inches below my crotch. One of my girlfriends called it a 'Greyhound Dress' since it was three inches from the hare (hair! Get it?). Second, it is the only dress I have worthy of the Altura.

I also had on my black spike heels. The combination of the dress and the heels made my legs look like a million bucks. I do have great looking legs. The dress also did very nice things for my ass too, even though I wouldn't have time to lose the extra weight that I needed to.

I tried to decide what jewelry to wear with the outfit. I'd gotten as far as picking a pair of earrings that were simple twoinch gold loops. I thought the earrings did an excellent job of giving me an enticing and sexy look with my new hairdo.

I paused in front of the mirror again. What did I know about this guy for sure other than he liked Starbucks? He could be a mass rapist or some kind of ax murderer that preyed on women my age? This could be the date from hell. I could have committed to the weekend from hell. What if his family were all looney tunes? Was my acceptance of this weekend just a flight of fancy for me that I'd regret all the rest of my days?

The doorbell rang. Ben was early? Did I have the time wrong?

I peeked through the eyepiece in my door, and there was a man with flowers, but not my man. I opened the door with the chain on.

"Delivery for Avery Hart," he smiled and held out a corsage box.

I adjusted the door and opened it all the way. Florist man handed me the box and wished me a good evening. I patted my dress as if looking for a pocket I knew I didn't have. "Don't bother," he said. "The tip has already been paid. An excellent tip has already been paid. An excellent tip, he's a keeper," with a smile, he turned and disappeared down the stairs of my building. I took the chilled white box into my living room and opened it. There was a beautiful orchid corsage, small and not too flashy, yet carefully crafted—all the evil thoughts about Ben vanished from my mind.

There was a small envelope with 'Avery' written on it. I opened it and read the enclosed card:

Avery

Pretty flowers for a much more stunning woman See you soon, girlfriend.

Ben.

My heart melted. Maybe I'd let this guy get lucky on our first date. What am I thinking?

I sat and smelled the flowers for five minutes. I decided I'd better stop, or there would be no more odor atoms on the flowers by the time we went for dinner. I went and touched up my makeup for the fortieth time that night and paced some more, now wearing the corsage pinned to my dress. I changed my earrings for the fifth time in the past half hour. My fake diamond studs replaced the hoops.

On the dot of seven-thirty, Ben knocked on the door. I opened it to find my handsome prince standing there in a very fashionable tuxedo. My God, the last time anyone had picked me up in a tuxedo was my high school senior prom. This man was scoring points he didn't even know about. I expected my mother would want photos of the event.

"Wow," he said. "You look magnificent. I think this may be the best date I've ever been on." His comment didn't betray even the slightest hint that he wanted to feed me a line.

More points, I thought.

"Come in for a minute," I said. "I'd show you the place, except you can see it all from where you're standing." Ben stood and gazed about my neatened studio. Everything was packed carefully in the vertical racks and bookcases. Not a cubic inch was wasted or empty, floor to ceiling. I was a packrat.

A few pieces of my own art that intrigued me decorated the walls. He asked about them, and I explained each piece briefly.

Finally, I picked up a paisley shawl, put it over the one shoulder that didn't have the flowers on it, and gestured to the door. We left and locked up.

I let Ben escort me down to his car that was doubleparked at the curb. His car turned out to be a vintage Porsche 944 Turbo.

"I've never ridden in a Porsche," I jumped up and down a little with glee. Ben laughed at me.

Fifteen minutes later, after entrusting the Porsche to a valet, we were seated in the posh amber glow of the restaurant. My chair had a velveteen finish on it, and I thought that I might do nothing but rub the edge of the chair all night long to enjoy the tactile sensation from the fabric.

Ben got us both chocolate martinis. Something I'd never tried before and after one sip declared as my new favorite drink. We were sitting side by side in a booth, and it allowed me to study Ben and touch his arm with little flirty gestures.

Ben apologized ahead of time for any infraction of manners that he might incur; "You have to understand that I haven't been on a real date in four years. The Foundation has taken up all of my time, so I just haven't felt I could leave it. I guess I'm a control freak, certainly about the Foundation."

I looked attentive and nodded encouragingly to hear him talk. He went on, "I think things are getting to where I could at least let them coast every now and then rather than feel that if I wasn't in personal control, things would fly apart. I guess I'm a control freak."

I admitted that I had control issues, too, particularly about the quality of the art and other studio work that my company produced for our clients. We bounced around talking about business.

Over appetizers, I asked, "Tell me your life philosophy? Also, you haven't told me what you told your family and friends about your girlfriend or me?"

Ben said, "Let me take the second question first. Under great duress and having had a tad too much wine, I told Victor, Jennifer, and Tiffany, my sibs, that I did too have a girlfriend but that you'd had to spend the holiday with your family outside Seattle somewhere. I think I said you had dark hair and a nice figure. I said you had your own business, so you'll have to waltz around how I got that wrong. I avoided saying what business you were in, and I told you I didn't give a name. You are just 'nameless girlfriend' to them." He laughed at some internal joke.

I said with a touch of sarcastic humor, "Well, you certainly spilled the beans and left them knowing all about me, didn't you?"

"I've always been brief." He thought and then said, "Oh, I did tell them you liked to jog and ski. So it's a good thing you opted for the ski day. I told them you volunteered, charitable work of some kind; that scores points in my family; it's one of the family values. I think I also said you were intellectual and liked to read a lot."

"Did you tell them how we met?" I asked.

"Tiffany, the one getting married, asked me that," Ben said.

"I told her we'd met at a party some mutual friends through Charles Schwab that handles the investments in the foundation."

I muttered under my breath, "Party, Schwab, investments," trying to memorize the small points to buttress Ben's white lie to Tiffany.

"You've mentioned your friends, but you haven't talked about them yet. What did you tell them?"

Ben continued between bites of a carefully cracked crab cocktail," A few of my five best friends may be around sometime over the weekend. All are my age, and we were in high school together. Tiffany invited them to the wedding, but I don't know if they're coming. Mike is now a flight instructor at a small airport outside Seattle. Adam is an insurance agent, and Will's a computer jock of some type. James's a marketing guy for Coors, and Steven is a software designer and consultant." "Are they married?" I asked.

"Yes, they're all married, and I seem to be the holdout. Lots of pressure on that front." Ben rolled his eyes skyward. "Your efforts will go a long way towards removing the stigma that has haunted me for years." He laughed at his own humor.

They must be thinking that maybe he's gay or something, I thought to myself.

Our entrees arrived with a grand flourish, and our conversation continued with me asking questions of Ben. To play the role of 'temporary girlfriend,' I figured there was a primary body of knowledge about each other that we should know.

As we talked, we shifted closer and closer to each other. I felt the flush of interpersonal chemistry with Ben, and from his attention, he did too.

We started to touch each other, first just small gestures to the other's sleeve or shoulder. Then we sought skin by a touch to the neck or face. I dusted a crumb from a dinner roll from Ben's cheek, surprising myself by letting my fingers linger a second longer than required.

As our dinner plates were cleared, Ben reached over and held my hand. There was no pretense, just a sincere wish to be in contact with me. I welcomed his advances. The chemistry got thicker.

Over coffee, I pulled Ben's arm around me. We were in a booth, and we both found comfort in my move.

At one point, I put my head on his shoulder and could feel him nuzzle his face into my hair. This dinner was suddenly going fast in the touching part, and I welcomed the speed.

I turned to him, and we kissed. We'd both wanted to kiss each other for the past hour at least. I would have kissed him Monday in front of *Starbucks*. Hell, I would have screwed him in front of *Starbucks* by Tuesday. Sorry but it's been a long time; I really need to get laid before we go.

Our first kiss became a noteworthy milestone in our new relationship. The growing affection and attraction we both felt for each other came through loud and clear.

Ben said, "Will you come back to my condo with me? You need to see it anyway before we go to Aspen."

I nodded my agreement, knowing that there would be further kisses and some decisions about how fast and how far this relationship was moving.

We kissed again and with greater frequency as we finished our coffees, and Ben settled the bill. The Porsche had been waiting at the door for our departure.

Chapter Four

The building with Ben's condo looked modest from the outside. However, the inside impressed me immediately. Hallways were spotless and carefully maintained.

Ben parked in a private garage under the building. A private elevator whisked us up to Ben's penthouse, and when the doors opened, and Ben flipped on a light switch, I instantly came to an abrupt stop taking in the great room. This was no little condo.

Ben nudged me further into the room as I twirled around, looking up at the high ceilings and approximately at the ultra-modern décor.

At one end stood a modern kitchen with granite counter tops. Modern lighting lit the room from every direction. Bar stools allowed guests to talk to the cooks while meals were being prepared. A thick glass top dining room table sat midway across the room, surrounded by robust swivel barrel chairs. The living room centered on a fireplace and hearth with modern sofas built into a conversation pit that guests descended into. A large glass coffee table was centered in the hole. Modern paintings decorated the walls here and there.

Tall windows filled the two exterior walls, each with a settee built into the window alcove. Outside through the darkness, I could see the lake and the moon's light on the water, and the stars gave a startlingly beautiful display.

Ben stood with evident pride as I marveled at the splendor of his condo.

"Oh, wow!" I muttered as we walked deeper into the room. I was in awe at the simple luxury of Ben's home.

Suddenly I realized the expense of what I was seeing and what it meant about Ben. I turned to him with a significant question on my face. I skipped about ten obvious questions and went right to "Why me?"

Ben came to me and held me by the shoulders at arm's length; one thumb lightly stroked my neck. "I like you. I think you like me. You have a beautiful smile. After talking to you all week, I know you are what I need." "The wedding?" I asked.

"We leave here at noon tomorrow if you're still willing?"

"Ben, you obviously come from money. I didn't realize it, but now the pieces fit. The Foundation, family foundation...your Foundation; the Porsche; and now this." I gestured about the condo. "I'm pretty poor, actually. I'm making about seventy thousand a year, and in my family, that's a record. When my parents retire, they'll need some of my financial help to get by.

College professors are not big breadwinners."

"Avery, please don't think about the economic differences between us. Please don't think of any differences between us. I know you're not a gold digger. I could tell after talking to you for five minutes. The rest I don't care about, and I don't want you to either."

Ben pulled me into him slowly, and I went quite willingly. We leaned into each other and kissed. This time it was one of those explosives, TNT packed kisses full of tremendous potential and loaded with promises of more incredible things to come.

Ben touched a control on the counter top, and the leading lights dimmed, leaving a few pieces of art spotlighted as well as a hallway that I assume went back to his bedroom. He touched another button on the control console, and the fireplace leaped into flames. He also shed the jacket and tie it to his tux, draping the coat over a dining room chair.

"Come," Ben said. He led me into the living room 'pit,' pulling me beside him on the sofa. As I snuggled against him, I remembered the flowers; I unpinned the corsage and put it on the glass coffee table; I didn't want it crushed. When I turned back to him, he held his arms open to me, and I melted into them.

Adult necking is exciting because you know sooner or later where it could lead. In this case, I really wanted to be seduced or to be the seductress. I didn't care; I just wanted to be loved by this man even as a 'temporary girlfriend.'

Ben was very proper about where to put his hands. He stroked my arms and my neck and, of course, was kissing me in those places too. After a while, I realized he was not going to make 'the' move. I also noticed that my skirt had ridden up almost to my hips, clearly exposing my little black lacy bikini underwear and the tops of my hose.

Eventually, as we were locked in a long French kiss, I took one of Ben's hands and moved it to my left breast.

The hand went to work immediately, bringing me pleasure, stroking and smoothing me through the material of the dress.

I know we could both feel my nipples harden to his touch. The more he touched, the more I was sure where I wanted this to go.

As we kissed again a few minutes later, I took Ben's hand and, this time, brought it to the skin above my stocking tops and below my black lace panties. Ben moaned his pleasure at my invitation.

I had had other lovers in my life that were more experienced, but they were also more presumptive. Ben did not assume anything about where we were going. I'm not sure he knew. I did.

As he stroked the skin and my thighs, I gave a little moan of pleasure too. I finally said, "You can touch me anywhere you want, Ben, anywhere. I give myself to you tonight."

Ben whispered, "That's a big responsibility, and I accept. I give myself to you too."

I thought I must be the luckiest girl in the whole world. Here I had this hunk of a guy who could be in movies, and instead, he was with me. Further, he was friendly and levelheaded and wasn't the dork that so many of the men I'd met recently seemed to be. He actually paid attention to me, and I didn't detect any of the negative traits that finally drove me to leave Bill.

Ben started to rub my pubic area through the lace panties. I could feel myself flood with juices in anticipation of going to bed with him. I know my attractive sexual odor was increasing through the night; I hoped it was working.

I reached over to Ben with one hand and rubbed his thighs up to their union with his groin. Beneath the pants, to his tuxedo, I could feel a firm bulge. I stoked with different levels of pressure and in other ways all around the area. Things grew more prominent and more rigid. I was impressed and wanted more.

We made better use of our hands and mouths now that I'd established the permissible landscape for travel everywhere.

Finally, I could stand it no longer and slowly stand in the dim light, the gas fire flickering behind me. Ben watched me with a questioning look on his face.

"Too many clothes," I said. "Let's get more comfortable." My tone of voice was imperative, demanding that he move into action. He quickly followed my lead.

I shimmied a little in front of Ben just to catch his attention and then magically lifted the little black dress up over my head. I stood in heels, dark stockings, bikinis, and push-up bra; I looked at Ben. He'd become mesmerized by my rapid strip and stopped removing his own clothing. I was actually pleased I could elicit a look of such awe from such a handsome guy.

I reached behind and slowly undid the clasp to the black lacy bra. I held the bra close to my chest with one hand as I let the back and sidepieces come to the front. Ben realized that only my one hand and the flimsy fabric covered my breasts. His eyes widened.

I dropped the lacy bra on the sofa next to Ben with a dismissive gesture. I rubbed my breasts then held them forward to him as eye candy and for his enjoyment. I felt unbelievably sexy and most definitely the seductress of the evening.

Ben quickly lost his shirt and started to work on his pants, at least getting them down to his knees as he sat on the low sofa. I leaned forward so I could kiss Ben, knowing that as I did, my two breasts would become pendulums swinging in the dim light for his enjoyment. I wanted to show off my wares. I wanted him to touch and feel me.

As we kissed, both of Ben's hands rose and held my breasts, carefully weighing and caressing each globe. His hands were warm and comfortable, kneading and fondling with just the right amount of pressure and attention.

As his hands shifted their attention to my nipples, I could feel the sensations shoot through my body. He had my nipples erect; I paid rapt attention to his every move.

We kissed again, and then I directed Ben's mouth to my breasts. I straddled Ben's hips but elevated my body, so my breasts were at the level of his mouth. He got the idea right away and started to suck on my breasts, alternately kissing, slavering, and sucking hard on and around each nipple.

"Oh my God, I've died and gone to heaven," The sensations were almost too much to bear...but I bore up under strain.

After a few minutes, I pulled away from Ben and pulled his pants down and off his legs. Socks went next. Then I reached for his briefs. I wanted to see exactly what was causing that large bulge in the dark fabric of his underwear.

Ben raised his hips as I pulled down the briefs, so I yanked the shorts down to his knees in one smooth move. Immediately his cock unfurled into view, uncurling almost like a flag captured by a sudden wind that moves from a small tuft of fabric into being a grand and glorious display. Such was my first impression of Ben's privates.

I knelt before Ben and pulled his briefs off the rest of the way, tossing them into the growing pile of our clothing.

My hands reached up and together encompassed Ben's penis, counter, twisting the growing rod of flesh in my hands. I could feel the surge of growth as Ben moaned into the darkness, his head lolling back on the sofa in ecstasy as I fondled him.

I'd learned about blowjobs in high school. At the time, they'd been more than a substitute for intercourse, plus the boys I dated usually were thoughtful enough to return the favor. Thus, over the years, I had not only developed a skill and facility for the act but a genuine fondness. Further, unlike many women, I actually appreciated the final act of ejaculation in my mouth. I enjoyed the look of lust and pleasure on a guy's face as I swallowed his emissions.

I leaned over Ben, initially wrapping his cock with my breasts. His head snapped forward from his reverie so he could watch what I was doing. I must admit, when I'd seen it in porn films, the act looks dirty and seductive, and I loved doing it. Ben liked it too, for he started moaning and expressing his appreciation.

After a few minutes of that, I slid his cock up my chest and neck and then glommed onto the mushroomed head with my mouth. Another loud moan came from deep within Ben's body.

I pumped with one hand and rose and fell over his unit with my head, my tongue rolling around the top of his cock to deliver maximum stimulation. I could feel the penis grow even more and harden as I gave my lust to him.

Occasionally, I pulled off of Ben completely and blew lightly on the saliva-soaked rod; as I did, I'd run a fingernail up and down the prominent veins. The texture of his cock grew to that of hardened steel.

I stood before Ben. He looked at me the lust that I had fully aroused in him. I liked this look. I carefully and seductively peeled my black bikini panties down my legs, retaining my sexy black nylons and spike heels. Someone had told me once that men love seeing a woman wearing heels while they fuck; something about increasing the erotic sight picture.

I ran my hands around my pussy, moving so Ben's head ended only a few inches from my ground zero. I ran two fingers of one hand into my vagina and pulled them out. I licked them then brought them to Ben's mouth. He licked.

Ben brought a hand up and ran it up the inside of my thigh. The touch was electric.

I felt like I was on fire. I held Ben's hand and directed it to my center. Two of his fingers penetrated my sopping vagina, my fluids flooding over as he made a few strokes in and out of me.

The whole time his fingers penetrated me, our eyes were locked on each other. I steadied myself with one hand on his shoulder as I rotated my hips to meet his touch.

Finally, I spoke, "Can you just fuck me? Please!".

Chapter Five

Ben rose from the sofa and faced me, his arms wrapped around me, and we kissed in the most intimate and yet loving kiss of the night.

Without warning, Ben picked me up and quickly carried me down the hallway I'd seen and had assumed led to the bedroom area. I was right.

Ben's bedroom was also dimly lit by low wattage spots on some of the artwork on the walls. The windows also faced the river and the light off the moon; spectacular view, but that wasn't why I'd come.

He set me gently on the bed and moved between my legs. I pulled my legs up to welcome his advance.

Ben thrust his tongue forward into my slit, licking and savoring all of the fluids I'd been leaking throughout the evening. I think the corsage had been the turning point. I'm a sucker for flowers.

This man knew his way around a woman's pussy, and he toured all over mine. Tongue and then fingers stroked, licked, and sucked in all the right places. My little tufts of sensitive skin found their way into his mouth with just the correct pressure and stimulation.

I soared ever higher until I could take it no more and clutched Ben's head to my nether region, and allowed my first orgasm of the night to wash over me.

My heart raced, my blood pressure must have skyrocketed, and I had the slight sheen of lust all over my body to celebrate the passing of that orgasm. Wow!

I pulled Ben up towards me. "Come to me, lover." He didn't need a second invitation.

Ben slid into my velvet sheath in one smooth stroke. Again, our eyes were locked on each other. This was a union we both sought with all our bodies, and as it would turn out our hearts.

I urged Ben's thrusts into me using my own abilities to rotate and thrust into his down strokes with my pelvis. We were hellbent on achieving more orgasms, and in only a few minutes, Ben warned of his impending climax.

"Come in me," I said. "I love you."

I thought, oh my God, I've said the 'L' word. What will he think? We are acting right, so this fits.

My words didn't seem to change Ben's ardor, and he continued to drive deeper into me with ever-faster strokes. I started to moan and add short stories of encouragement.

"Cum.Fill me.Fuck me.Shoot into me.Ooooooooooh . Ooooooooh fuuuuccccccckkkkkk!"

I was holding off my own climax to await Ben's. When he started to make his final lunges into my body, I gave in to what my body had been pleading for release.

We both exploded into each other. I could feel the jets of Ben's ejaculations washing down the inside of my vagina. Every nerve ending in my sheath was afire with pleasure as I spasmed around his spike.

For half a minute, we were statue frozen in time. Our hearts beat, yet no one breathed or moved. We just savored the pleasure of the orgasms that touched us both.

Then we both gasped for air, and I pulled Ben down into my arms, cradling his head on my shoulder.

"Wow," he whispered to me as we both panted.

"Yeah," I said, "Wow."

We were both silents after those assertions. I guess we were both unsure what to say. Where to take the conversation, or even whether a discussion was needed.

We were both lightly stroking each other; Ben was running a finger lazily around my right breast. The sensation was delightful. I was stroking his arm with one hand and touching his hair with my other hand.

After several minutes I broke the silence. "Ben, thank you. You are a heavenly lover."

That was a stupid thing to say, I thought. Ben's going to think I'm crazy.

He leaned in and kissed me. "And you, dearest Avery, are an adorable surprise and a delight."

My heart went all flippy-floppy again. I am also a sucker for being adored.

I spent the night with Ben. We made love again. In the morning, Ben awakened me with lots of kisses, my kind of alarm clock.

In the bold light of day, we both looked at each other full of questions about whether the previous night has been an irregularity. Ben looked at me between his initial kisses. After my eyes were open with his eyebrows peaked over the brow of his beautiful nose. They were sort of asking if this whole situation was all right or whether I wanted to run screaming out the door.

To remove that stigma, at least from my point of view, I pulled Ben to me after his second or third kiss and said, "You can make love to me like you did last night any time you want while we are gone. For me, that was the perfect date. You are the perfect date. I like being your 'temporary girlfriend.'" Then I kissed his nose.

I turned so I could kiss him better and pulled him into me. We were both still nude, and I quite purposefully pulled the sheet down my body to reveal my breasts to Ben and the rays of early morning sunshine. Secretly too, I hoped he'd make some statement removing the stigma of 'temporary' from my status.

Ben responded, well, my kind of man. We made love again, but he made no comment about us getting more serious.

After the two of us showered together in his luxurious bathroom, I stumbled around the living room, collecting my clothing and redressing. I stuck the stockings in a grocery store bag along with the shawl and somehow got back into the rest of the things I'd been wearing. Ben dressed more casually and appeared just as I slid the LBD down over my body.

"Such a shame to cover up such beauty," he said, and he came and took me in his arms again.

"Oh, I bet you say that to all the girls you entertain here."

Ben looked at me seriously and said, "Other than the family, you are the first woman that has been here the way we were last night. I meant what I said about having been a loner for a long time."

"Well, Mr. Loner, you did pretty well last night by me. I may not be all that experienced either, but I know that you turned me on and kept turning me on, and well, you're still turning me on."

We kissed again, and then I pushed him off.

"You have to take me home so I can be ready for our flight to Colorado. By the way, what time is our flight? What airline?"

Ben looked a little pleased with himself; he said, "I'll drive you home. The trip is a bit of a surprise so, just go with the flow. Okay?"

I nodded to accept his edict...

Chapter Six

Ben and I went down to the garage and got into his Porsche. A few minutes later, he'd negotiated the backstreets of Seattle and delivered me to my door with the promise to be back at noon to take me to the airport.

He told me we'd have lunch on the plane.

I thought it odd that he told me to bring whatever I thought I'd need, including bulky winter coats. He said it'd all go fine on the plane one way or the other and that he'd help me carry it all.

I had a pile of luggage on the door stoop at noon, and Ben double-parked as we loaded it all into the back of the Porsche.

I ended holding a few things on my lap.

As we pulled away from my apartment, I noted that Ben was headed in the opposite direction from Seattle Airport.

"What gives? Where are you taking me?" I asked.

Ben smiled and said, "Remember, just go with the flow. You'll like it. I promise."

I feel like I'm back in the *Fifty Shades of Grey* book again. I relaxed and enjoyed Ben's skills at negotiating the expensive and fast car onto the freeway like it was no problem at all. I hate getting on the highway. Eventually, I figured out we were going to the airport in Port Angeles, Washington. It's a general aviation airport with a few flights and some personal flights from time to time. The field used to be a military base.

Ben wheeled into the general aviation side of the field, pulling up in front of a large electric gate and pushing a button on the car's visor to have the gate open for us. As we drove through, we passed row upon row of single-engine private planes.

Ben then turned abruptly and pulled up next to a sleek corporate jet. I noticed the tail number on the plane was B1CF. I looked at Ben, full of questions.

"My plane," he explained tersely. My mouth fell open again. My 'boyfriend' owned a corporate jet! Oh, my God. This is so *Fifty Shades of Grey*. Now I'm thinking of the sex we had. Was he playing with me and is really like *Mr. Grey*?

Ben saw my look of awe and added, "Actually, the plane belongs to the Foundation. That's why the 'CF' is part of the tail number. It stands for Case Foundation."

As I walked around the sleek jet, a lineman carried our luggage from the car to the plane. Ben asked him to put the car on the hanger. The man drove carefully away towards the enormous vacant hanger that had apparently housed the jet until sometime this morning.

"Who's going to fly this," I asked since there was no one else around.

"I am," Ben said with a widening smile. "Come on, let's get in and get going."

Ben helped me up the stairs and into the jet. I started to head towards the passenger seats in the rear, but Ben pulled my arm.

"Come and sit up front with me. You'll be my co-pilot today." Ben turned and secured the door to the plane after the stairs folded away automatically.

I think my jaw was hanging open again. Yes, I am in that book. If I see a room of red, I'm running for dear life.

"I don't know...you don't expect...are you sure..." I started blabbering.

Ben stopped me by waving his hand at the plane. "This is a Cessna Citation Ultra. It was built in 1999, and I've owned it since 2004. The engines are almost new. We will cruise at about 40,000 feet and go directly from here to Aspen, Colorado, at a distance of 835 nautical miles. The flight will take about two hours and twenty-nine minutes at a speed of 456 knots, give or take a little for winds at altitude."

He helped me into the co-pilot's seat and showed me how to attach the five-point harness. He also showed me the quickdonning oxygen mask and a few of the other safety features about the plane. He explained that the aircraft had a small head if I needed relief as well as a tiny galley that had been stocked with sandwiches, soft drinks, and coffee for our flight. That song from the movie called *Earned It* by *The Weekend* came into my head. "*Love you like I do...*"

"Did you say something?"

"No, just thinking of a song," with that, Ben finished attending to his own seat and starting touching dials and levers. Almost immediately, the entire instrument panel before me lit up. A minute later, I heard an engine spool up behind us. Three LED displays appeared. Ben put a headset on and apparently was listening to something on the radio. He handed me a lightweight headset and said, "Here, put this on. You'll be able to talk to me better and hear both sides of my conversation with air traffic control. Just don't talk while they are, Okay?" I nodded, still awed by all going on around me. So much like the movie. I thought.

Ben adjusted the frequencies on one of the radios. I heard him say through my headset, "Port Angeles Clearance, Bravo

One Charlie Foxtrot at Hanger Two, ready for our clearance to Aspen, Colorado, alpha sierra echo."

After thirty seconds, the radio sparked to life, "Citation Bravo One Charlie Foxtrot, you are cleared to alpha sierra echo as filed. After takeoff, climb and maintain the runway heading to four thousand. Contact ground on one-two-one point seven when ready to taxi."

Ben repeated the clearance instructions back. He touched one of the radios, changing frequencies, and then I heard him tell Fairchild ground control that he was ready to taxi.

The tower responded immediately, "Citation Bravo One Charlie Foxtrot cleared to taxi to runway two-niner. Contact building on one-one-eight-point-five when ready for takeoff.

With great excitement, the engines got louder, and the large aircraft started to move. I had a smile from ear to ear, and so did Ben. I noticed the lineman outside the plane waving with two batons as we turned and left the hanger area. I waved a little 'thank you' to the guy.

We rolled slowly down one of the taxiways. Ben explained that he had checklists for everything. We'd spend a minute at the end of the runway going through the pretakeoff list and then let the tower know we were ready for departure.

At the end of the runway, Ben parked the plane and pulled out a laminated card. He vocalized each checklist item as he went through it, often pointing to an instrument or lever around him to confirm its setting. After two minutes with the checklist and setting some information in some of the instruments. I heard his voice on the headset again, "Port Angeles Tower, Bravo One Charlie Foxtrot is ready for takeoff."

The radio again came to life, "Citation Bravo One Charlie Foxtrot, hold short of two-niner." Ben acknowledged the contact. In another minute, the radio came to life again; Citation

Bravo One Charlie Foxtrot cleared for takeoff; runway heading to four thousand."

The plane turned slowly out of the run-up area and made a ninety-degree turn onto the runway. When the plane was right on the center line, Ben pushed the throttles forward, and I could hear the two jet engines wind up behind us.

Then suddenly we were hurtling down the runway, and just as suddenly, he rotated the plane's nose into the air, and we were airborne.

Ben's hands flew around the cockpit for a few seconds. I heard a communication from the tower, "Citation Bravo One Charlie Foxtrot, contact departure on one-two-one-point-four, good day." Ben repeated the instruction and bid Fairchild Field goodbye.

He contacted departure, and they cleared him direct to Aspen and up to seventeen thousand feet just like that. We rose rapidly, and I watched the earth slip away beneath us. As we approached seventeen thousand feet (Ben showed me how to read the altimeter), Departure Control handed us off to Seattle Center. Center immediately cleared us to flight level four-zero-zero. The radios then got amazingly silent as we finished our climb to altitude.

I'd been remarkably silent through the entire takeoff and climb. Now I finally told Ben, "So I am unbelievably impressed by all this. I bet you're trying to get into my pants." I grinned at him.

He grinned back and said, "Nope. Been there; done that. Plus, you told me I could have you anytime I want."

"So, can we talk now?"

"Not until you open up the door to galley and get our two box lunches and a coke for me and whatever you want to drink." I pushed my seat back, made my way to the galley area, and served the captain his lunch. The deli sandwiches were superb.

As we were near altitude, Ben nodded and pointed outside my window. A couple of thousand feet below us a mountain and blue sky. I felt like I could reach out and grab the clouds from the sky. I grinned again. This was amazing.

I began, "I asked about your philosophy on life, love, and happiness, or something like that. We got sidetracked, and I'd still like to hear it."

"Tall order," he said. "I had thought about it when you weren't otherwise distracting me. Which has become most of the time in a very nice way. Let me talk about it unless I have to talk to ATC, and then you can ask questions." I nodded.

Ben began, "Okay, first about family. I think my family is essential. I feel close to my brother and sisters, and we all talk at least once a week, sometimes three or four times a week, so they must feel that way too. Our discussion is about the Foundation, but we are open about how we think about each other, and I think we are supportive. There are no hidden feelings, although I feel guilty for hiding my social status. If I believe Victor, my brother, is being a dork, I tell him and vice versa. That is why they're all riding me so hard about being my age without a serious girlfriend.

The headphones squawked, and a voice said, "Citation Bravo One Charlie Foxtrot, contact Seattle Center on a one-three-two-decimal-two-five, good day."

Ben's voice immediately answered, "Over to Seattle for Charlie Foxtrot, Good day Fairchild." I watched Ben push a button and heard his voice again; "Seattle, Bravo One Charlie Foxtrot with you at flight level four-zero-zero." ATC responded, and the radio went quiet also.

Ben picked up the thread of his comments about life; "I guess I should preface all of this by saying that I think you have to like yourself first. If you don't like who you are, fundamentally, I don't think you can have good relationships with anyone.

I don't mean you have to be narcissistic, but you do have to believe that you're fundamentally okay."

He went on, "As far as relationships, I'm jaded by what I've seen around me and how I think things should work. Divorce rates and break-ups seem to be the norm, at least for a lot of people. The way we conceive of marriage or manwoman relationships just doesn't work. I think I might know why, but

it'll be a reach for you, I'm sure." "Try me," I said.

"Well, we've been programmed to be monogamous, only couples allowed. I think that's an artificial rule someone five thousand years ago thought up to control women's abuse or to stabilize the tribe or something. The idea is outmoded today."

"Why is it outmoded?" I asked, curious about where this was going. But I felt like the other shoe just dropped.

"Well, how many people could you love at once?" Ben asked.

"No fair," I replied, "there are different kinds of love; parent, child, family, friend, lover, just to toss out a few."

"No, stick with 'lover' because that's where the kind of relationships we're talking about happens. The rest is excellent, even necessary, but how many people could you love?"

I thought for a minute and said, "In theory, I could have several lovers at the same time. Whether I'd want to or could handle all the interactions is debatable."

Ben said, "Just assume you could. You could have a serious relationship with more than one person, two, three, possibly four before you got stressed out. So why would you do this? What would you get from the other people that you don't get from your 'one'?"

I responded, "I'm assuming we love each other and that they'd be different people. Our interactions would be different. They'd see the world differently from each other. They'd each like different things and come at problems differently."

"If you are going to grow, evolve, and personally develop, there might be some significant advantage to being in love with more than one person?"

I nodded slowly, agreeing with his thesis.

"Now, I toss this in for free. Do all the people that you love have to be men?"

"No, definitely not," I replied.

"Sexual relationships?" he asked.

"In your philosophy, it would be 'whatever works,' right? Men or women." I said.

Ben nodded and asked, "Have you?"

I nodded. "Once, in college. It was more an experiment than any type of flaming love affair, although we both learned and grew as a result. I've heard other people call it being a LUG." Ben looked puzzled; I explained, "Lesbian until graduation," I explained. He laughed.

"Did you date?"

"Oh, I was Miss Social Butterfly in high school and college.

I got more serious in graduate school. Except for one college roommate a few times, I am pure heterosexual. My dalliance with her let me postpone having a serious boy-girl relationship at the time." I paused and added, "Go back to your philosophy."

Chapter Seven

Ben thought for a moment as he adjusted a few controls on the jet. He went on, "I like the idea of polyamory or a loving group of people that have negotiated their intimate life together. Their sensitivity to the currencies they 'pay' each other with. You can't be jealous; that's a learned emotion anyway. You can't 'own' another person; you deal with others in adult-adult relationships. There's no mandated exclusivity. You have to start on that premise, and then you can build a relationship or family of relationships."

He went on, "Everyone is committed to everyone else's joy and growth. Every day you look out for the others and ask yourself, how can I love this person today…and this person…and this person? You do things to keep the magic in the whole extended family. You take pleasure in watching the others you love being pleasured. And if there's conflict, your first thought is, how can we create a 'win' for both of us?

The radio squawked, "Citation Bravo One Charlie Foxtrot contact Boise Airport on one-three-two-decimal-five." Ben acknowledged the hand off and called into the new air traffic control center.

Ben reached across the cockpit and took my hand. He brought it to his mouth, kissed my palm, and closed my fingers around it, and then set my hand back in my lap. I know I blushed at his tender gesture.

We were both silent for a moment. Ben then said, "See. You get the idea," Ben said. He thought for a minute and asked, "Tell me about you and exercise?"

"Let's go back to the last subject for a minute. Have you been in a relationship like this before?"

"Yes, and it ended after three months because a couple of people got jealous. It fell apart after that, and I've met up with one or two of them, but it never felt the same. Tell me about you and exercise,"

"That's an embarrassing question," I said. "I exercised all through college and grad school, and now I always seem to have an excuse."

"Will you jog with me and work out?"

"I'd love to if you don't put me to shame with your superior body." I reached over and lightly squeezed his biceps with two fingers. "In case you didn't notice, I need to lose twenty pounds." He ignored my comment.

"I meditate when I exercise," he said. "Somehow, when I'm running, I tune in to my breathing, and then I feel nothing at all other than a sense of unity within and connections to everything. I meditate other times too, irregular schedule, I'm afraid. A rewarding activity, I find." "Will you teach me?" I asked.

Ben chuckled and said, "I will be delighted. The thought of meditating is perhaps a good meditation, or you can just focus only on your footsteps don't even count."

The radio crackled again, and Ben handled a frequency change. He pointed out the distant city of Salt Lake City off to our right as we coasted by. The weather was crystal clear over Utah.

Ben said, "One of the things we haven't really talked about is why we do the things we do, for instance, why am I running the Case Foundation? We talked about how I made the whole portfolio thing, stocks, bonds, and investments but not the other side of things."

"So why?" I asked with a wise ass smirk.

"As my long-time girlfriend, you have to know this; somewhere deep in me is an ever-present voice that says I have to give to others. It's not religious; it's spiritual, perhaps it's even guilted having so much in such a needy world. It's also a family mission, to try to uplift people in unique ways around the communities we live in and around the world and make it stick."

"Like cure world hunger?" I asked more seriously.

"I'd love to, but that's a sinkhole for money. We're trying to come at issues like that but more creatively like education programs, establishing schools, rebuilding a hospital, establishing a bank that gives micro-loans, and so forth."

"How much do you donate or fund each year?"

"The Foundation donated over two hundred and fifty million. With our investments, we've been able to preserve the principle, even grow it a little, and invest about eight percent of that a year, twenty million."

I sat stunned at the magnitude of the Case Foundation. I knew I was traveling in good company. I looked at Ben with new awe, but he didn't see my look.

Our discussion wandered around the mechanics of the Foundation and how various causes were identified and funded. As we talked, I saw how the family often came together on conference calls to decide on programs and funding. He mentioned that several to do friends of his parents had donated large sums of money to the Foundation after they appreciated its goals and management.

"Ben, you are amazing. You are so unpretentious, and then you come along and sweep a girl off her feet with all this." I gestured to the airplane.

He shrugged and explained, "I spend at least a couple of days a week looking at where and how we can invest the Foundation's money to get bang for the buck, as they say. Most of the flights I make with this plane are in the United States. Still, we also have programs in the Middle East, Africa, India, and Malaysia's backwaters. Sometimes I'm gone for a couple of weeks." "Do you travel all that way alone?" I asked.

"No, we have a couple of pilots we can call on to rotate duties on the long-haul trips. We also add wing-tip fuel tanks that bring the range on the Citation up to about five thousand nautical miles. We need those for trips to Europe and beyond.

I was glad Ben had other help on the long trips. When I'd been overseas, the jet lag alone unfocused my mind so much, I couldn't imagine flying an airplane with that infirmity.

The radio came to life again, and we were handed off to Aspen Pikin Country. I was following our route on a map that Ben had given me. It had been interesting until a layer of clouds obscured my view of the ground.

Suddenly a wave of horniness swept over me. I looked at Ben. He was all business and reviewing one of his checklists.

"Honey? Hey, do you like being called 'Honey'?" I asked.

"Yes, dear," he said with a smirk.

"Honey, are you on autopilot?" "Yes, dear," he said with a mocking voice.

"Can we join the Mile-High Club?" I posed.

Ben's head snapped around, and he looked at me with his mouth hanging open. "I've never ...I don't think...well..."

I said, "In other words, it's not out of the realm of possibility?" He nodded dumbly, and a lustful look came over his face.

"Push your seat back," I commanded.

Ben slid the pilot's seat back about eighteen inches. He could still reach the controls, but space opened up a nice area where I could work some magic.

"Be right back," I said. I set my seat back and went to the small washroom and retrieved a couple of towels, and got a massive soft cushion I'd seen tossed on the sofa in the back of the plane. I also removed my underwear.

I went back in the cockpit and got back in my seat but sideways so I could lean across the console. I reached over and unzipped Ben's slacks. I was overly inefficient about finding and removing his inflating penis through his pants. Ben unbuckled his belt and shifted the pants down his body to help my apparent bumbling. The bumbling had really been on purpose. I bet he really liked having me feel him in all those different ways and positions.

At one point, I sat upright and pulled the blouse from my body. The bra went next. I looked out the windows and asked rhetorically, "Do you suppose the neighbors can see?" Ben appreciated my humor. One of his hands came and fondled the nearest breast.

I reached back and slowly masturbated Ben. As I did, he reached across with both hands and started to massage and tweak my breasts and nipples. Soon we both had each other panting for more significant sexual contact. Ben's rod pointed towards the sun.

"Can I mount you?" I asked, looking at all the controls.

"Yea, I think with the seatback this far. Just don't bump the control wheel. Come around the console."

I pulled my skirt down my legs and revealed to Ben that I was now totally nude in the co-pilot's seat. I struck a sexy and very revealing pose. "This is so whenever you fly this plane again, you'll always remember your favorite co-pilot."

I moved out from the seat and wiggled by the console and onto Ben's lap, facing him. He immediately sucked my right breast into his mouth. I moaned.

I masturbated Ben again, rubbing his swelling cock against my slit.

After only a few seconds of that kind of foreplay, I judged him ready for penetration, and I rose and directed him into my pussy. I pushed down slowly so we could both enjoy every fraction of an inch of his cock sliding into my body.

Ben uttered, "Oh shit, this is nice." I moaned even louder as his cock bottomed out against my cervix.

I moved above his body since he was severely motion restricted. He massaged my breasts with his hands and guided my hips up and down on his rod.

I pulled away and looked him in the eye. He looked back, and we kissed passionately.

"Welcome to the Club," I said. We both grinned at each other.

"I'm not going to last too long," he warned.

"Neither am I. Just cum in me. I want your juice."

Then we were there. Ben yanked my body down on his with four powerful downstrokes and then froze. I felt his cum shoot into me, and I came with just that single sensation. I arched back, careful not to disturb the flight controls.

We kissed each other passionately, all-around face, neck, ears, lobes, breasts, and shoulders, anything we could reach.

Our tongues probed deep into each other's mouths, tasting and sharing. The whole time we were groaning and moaning.

Suddenly Ben sat upright. "Wait," he said to me. He pulled the headset microphone back down in front of his mouth and said, "Bill, Boise. Could you repeat that frequency?" After a second, he repeated, "Okay, over to Salt Lake City on one-three-threepoint-seven-five. Thanks, and good day."

We both broke up laughing. Ben reached forward again to the microphone button and checked in with Salt Lake City. I noticed his voice had a distinctive edge to it as well as a little pant.

I reached across to my seat and retrieved the hand towels I brought. I gave one to Ben to catch his soggy penis as I pulled off of him. I clutched the other towelette to my full pussy as I rose.

In what was far from a graceful maneuver, I somehow twisted and turned around Ben and dismounted without touching any of the plane's equipment. I shuffled off towards the rear of the plane to clean up. I told Ben, don't go anywhere; I'll bring you a wet washcloth to help you clean up.

Five minutes later, I returned to the cockpit, only wearing the bikini underwear that I had packed. I leaned in, kissed Ben very tenderly, and then passed him a makeshift washcloth and watched as he wiped himself clean of our juices.

"I could help," I offered, purposely running my tongue over my lips in a very suggestive manner.

"Later," he smiled at me. He hitched his pants up and re-dressed himself, awkward in a seated position. When he was through, he secured his seat back into its regular position.

I gave Ben one more kiss, turned and retrieved my bra, blouse, and skirt, and went into the back of the plane again to redress. I also took the opportunity to touch up my makeup and hair that had become mussed in all the excitement.

A few minutes later, I went back to the cockpit. I kissed Ben and said, "Thank you. For taking something off my bucket list."

"You just wanted to be a member of the Mile-High Club," he said in a matter-of-fact voice.

"Were you already a member?" I asked, interested in his response.

"No, but I sure am now," he grinned.

"Thank you, honey." I stroked his cheek.

I put the headset on just in time to hear Denver Center come online. "Citation Bravo One Charlie Foxtrot descend and maintain flight level two-four-zero," Ben replied and made one small adjustment to a dial on the panel.

Instantly, I could feel the plane smoothly nose over and start to descend.

Chapter Eight

The cloud deck disappeared about ten minutes later, and I could look ahead and see the Rocky Mountains.

They were spectacular, with many of the higher peaks still carrying some snow. Ben pointed out Aspen ahead of us. Gradually we came to the foothills and then were deep over the Rockies.

ATC also had us descend further, gave us some vectors, got us to the approach course for Aspen's runway 33, and soon I watched as Ben executed a flawless landing in Aspen. I noticed we used most of the runway to land and stop. We taxied back towards one of the hangers.

A lineman directed us to the parking slot. Almost immediately, another lineman drove a rental car right next to the Citation jet. Ben went through the shutdown checklist as a lineman, and I put our things in the car.

When he was through with the plane, Ben went into the Atlantic Aviation office, checked in for the car, and decided to refuel the jet and stay for our overnights. He also arranged catering for the flight back to Seattle.

As I looked around at the surrounding mountains, I couldn't help but notice the absence of snow. When Ben came out of the office, I pointed and asked, "Are you sure we're going to ski on Monday?"

He frowned and said, "Perhaps we'll have to come up with some other kind of aerobic activity. You're right. I think the ski season is over." His mood then brightened, and he held the car door for me; did he ever have a bad day?

Ben drove out of the airport and got on the main highway for a short distance before turning off and snaking his way up a winding mountain road. I was captivated by the dramatic homes and then saw one that took my breath away near the top of a ridge. I pointed it out to Ben.

He smiled and said, "That's where we're going. I jointly own it with my brother and sisters. It's called Chateau Eagle Pines."

I think my mouth was hanging open again. It seemed to do that a lot with Ben.

As we turned into the mountain estate, I couldn't help but notice how the house was landscaped into the mountain to make it less obtrusive. Also, natural woods and stone had been used. That said, the home was palatial and extended equally on either side of a majestic circular driveway and entryway.

Ben led me into the home. Inside the house was just as impressive, an impressive mix of wood, stone, Navajo art, and contemporary furniture, all with muted tones to not overshadow the house's elegance.

Ben yelled, "Hellooooooo! Anyone home?"

The high vaulted ceilings had attracted my attention when a woman's voice shouted with glee. "BEN!" They're a pretty light brunette hurled herself into Ben's arms, locking both arms and legs around his body in a near smothering hug as he swung her around. Ben looked most pleased with his welcome.

The pair kissed and hugged again, and he set her down and turned her towards me.

"Tiffany, this is my girlfriend, Avery. Avery, this is my sister Tiffany and the cause of this wonderful celebration this weekend."

I put my hand out to shake her hand, but Tiffany would have none of that. She came to me and said, "We are a hugging family. Body contact is important." With that, the two of us hugged. It wasn't a girlie hug either; we made fullbody contact, and then she kissed me.

"Welcome to Eagle Pines," Tiffany said. "Come and let me get to know you better. You are so pretty. Ben barely told us anything about you at Christmas, so this is such a treat that you could come to the wedding." She cast a smiling frown at her brother. She added, "he's not the most communicative person either unless it involves the Foundation."

We followed Tiffany, who I rapidly learned was often just called 'Tiff,' into a massive kitchen with a sit-down counter. Tiff gestured, and we each took a seat. Tiff went to get us something to drink. Still, before anything else could happen, another brunette blur ran into the kitchen and threw herself into Ben's arms with another flurry of more kisses and hugs.

Ben extricated himself from the clingy female and said, "Avery, this furball of activity is my other sister Jennifer, and like Tiffany, she thinks I walk on water." "You wish we did," Jennifer said.

"Now that they are meeting you, they will surely think the same of you. I shall be forever demoted to more mundane human status as you are elevated to the status of Goddess."

Jennifer came to me, "Avery, I am so glad to meet you. I wish I could say I knew a lot about you, but Ben has kept you a secret from us all. We weren't really sure you even existed until today."

I made a note to myself to try not to spill the beans about my sudden relationship with Ben.

I hugged Jennifer as I met her halfway in her welcome. I also got a kiss from her too and a big welcome into the family. I liked this family; they were all touchy-feely.

I said in a conspiratorial tone, "Sometimes Ben even keeps it a secret from me that I'm his girlfriend. You must tell me all his deep and darkest secrets this weekend." I gave him a suspicious glance, and we all laughed.

I learned the two sisters had been up at the house from their homes in Denver since the start of the week consulting with various local places about the wedding. Victor, Ben's brother, his wife, and Jennifer's husband were due in on a commercial flight from Denver just in time for dinner. Other members of the bridal party, including the groom-to-be and his parents, stayed down in the romantic little town at one of the resorts.

Both Tiffany and Jennifer were short but thin brunettes. There was no doubt they shared the same parents and inherited the good looks from each side. However, I think they'd both had breast enhancements since they seemed a little rounder and more erect than one might expect. Both were happy and secure in who they were, and both adored Ben, their 'big' brother.

Ben was a year older than Jennifer and three years older than Tiffany. Victor was the youngest by another year.

I learned the wedding was to be at three o'clock on Saturday afternoon at the Elkhorn Lodge in Aspen, followed by a reception at the exclusive resort. Apparently, over three hundred guests were coming for the event. That evening, Tiffany informed us we were part of a rehearsal and then a large family dinner at the Century Room in the Hotel Jerome.

Suddenly Ben's sisters swept me up and spirited me away to one of the upstairs bedrooms to help dress for dinner and have 'girl talk.' Ben followed closely behind with my suitcase and clothes bag. He showed me the room that we'd claim for our visit, and then he disappeared. Our room held a kingsize bed and an assortment of new, woodsy furniture that fit the house's décor. The view out the window was spectacular. I loved the Rocky Mountains.

I got my little black dress and makeup kit and joined Ben's sisters a couple of doors down the hallway in Tiffany's bedroom. We all stripped down to our underwear and started to dress more upscale for the dinner and rehearsal. At the same time, we continued some girls chatter they'd already started before our arrival about the wedding, honeymoon, and much to my surprise, their sex lives. The sisters were incredibly open with each other, and I learned a lot from their conversation. Turned out they were learning things about each other for the first time too.

The discussion turned to some of the more exciting places they'd had sex in their lives. Jennifer talked about doing 'it' under stadium bleachers during a football game, the backseat of a car, a rocky tor along a frequented hiking trail, and in the ladies' restroom of a popular Denver pick-up bar called Blue 67. I listened to her condensed descriptions about how Jennifer, Melissa, and later Brad had almost gotten caught over and over again.

As Tiffany tried various cocktail dresses from her closet. She talked about how she had recently given Marc, her fiancé, a blowjob under the table at an upscale jazz joint called '1515'. Apparently, several others at the table knew of her efforts and applauded as Jennifer finished and arose from her under-the-table efforts with a small telltale sign on her cheek. She laughed uproariously as she remembered the event.

As she and Jennifer swapped clothes and went from near-nude to clothed and back to their nearly nude state, I actually felt my temperature rise. They were making me horny.

Suddenly they both turned to me, and I realized I had to 'stand and deliver' as the saying goes. I figured I'd surprise Jennifer and Tiffany a little.

"Well, up until today, I was not a member of the Mile High Club, but somewhere over Boise, Idaho. As we flew here, I stripped down to my necklace, and over Pocatello, I mounted Ben and sorted out that missing piece of my life with your brother," I began. "He told me it was his first time in the Club too. My God, can he fuck! I think we lasted all the way across the state and into Denver. Good thing the jet has an autopilot. I can't wait for our return trip. Maybe we'll try to last for four or five states instead of one and a half."

I turned to both girls with an innocent look on my face to see their mouths agape at my candid portrayal of our trip earlier in the day. Not to mention their witnessing a dimension of their brother that they hadn't thought about.

"That is so hot," Tiffany said. "I didn't think Ben had it in him."

Jennifer added, "I know he's well endowed. I saw him naked once a few years ago when he visited us in Denver. I 'accidentally' walked in on him when he was about to shower. Avery, you are so lucky...plus that all sounded like fun too."

"Well, your stories inspire me, although I'm not sure I have as many risk genes that you men apparently do." I began. "I would be mortified if I got caught, for instance, in a restaurant or at a football game." I thought for a moment, "But you men could do it on the airplane sometime, couldn't you?"

"Yeah," Jennifer said thoughtfully, "but it'd be no fun doing it with your husband. Maybe we should do it with Ben?" I refused to rise to the bait.

"Oh, that would be so nice. You men love each other and already touch and kiss more than in many families. Just extend what you're doing a little and bingo. Ben is so thoughtful about making sure you cum. Have you men ever done Ben, perhaps in a threesome or more some?" I asked them.

Jaws dropped, both at my casual attitude about their potential incest and at my suggestion of family love. I actually thought I wouldn't mind a lesbian-like encounter with either sister or both of them.

There was a long silence, and then I could hold in my laughter no longer. I burst out laughing.

"It's okay, men. You're brother's a hunk. Even though you're related, you can still lust after him. I bet half the women in Seattle do, and the other half haven't met him yet. And you don't have to answer my last question."

Both girls relaxed a little and grinned.

Tiffany finally said, "You knew we were playing with you?"

"Of course," I said. "Just put that on your to-do list. I won't stand in your way."

I still thought the whole discussion worth a laugh. Jennifer and Tiffany acted shocked again.

After a long silence, Jennifer volunteered in a voice just above a whisper, "I've had a threesome, actually I have had a foursome.

Brad and another couple we really like; we started a couple of months ago. We get together a couple of times a week, actually."

I looked at her with interest. I'd just learned a lot about Ben's sister, and more than he knew, I was sure.

Tiffany's jaw was hanging open at her sister's admission.

Then a grin started to spread from ear to ear.

"Why, Jen, you never shared that, and I have about a thousand questions," Tiffany paused. And alternately looked at the two of us as she tested our receptiveness to her next announcement; "Well, let me tell you that Marc and I have a lover too.

She actually lives with us and is one of my bridesmaids Melissa." She checked her watch and added, "Unless I'm wrong, I bet that Marc has his cock buried in her nice pussy even as we sit here. I hope they're both enjoying their time together." She grinned.

Now Jennifer's mouth was hanging open, and I think mine was too. Damn!

Tiffany went on, "I'll tell you another secret. Melissa is going on the honeymoon with us. No one else knows, so don't either of you dare tell anyone. We're all flying down to Puerto Vallarta on Sunday morning and intend to fuck each other's brains out all week."

Jennifer asked, "How long?"

Tiffany answered as she reached forward and took her sister's hand, then went and took my hand as well; "We fell in love almost two years ago. Actually, Marc and I were dating then, and one-night, Melissa needed a place to crash rather than drive home. We both knew her well and so having her stay over at our place was no big deal. One thing led to another and... well, we all fell in love with each other. Marc will be my husband and Melissa, my wife. Someday I hope we can make our triad legal; in the meantime, we'll just do what we do."

I squeezed Tiffany's hand as a gesture of support and appreciation for her revelations.

"What about Ben? Don't you want to share your story with him?" I asked quietly. "And Victor?"

Tiffany said, "You find a way to tell Ben. You are his girlfriend and understand him better than we do today. I'll have to see about telling Victor; he's pretty wrapped up in his own life right now. I know Victor has a stick up his butt about what a relationship like this would mean for the company. I think he's pretty conservative about everything." I nodded and wondered how and when I'd tell Ben.

Tiffany turned to her sister and asked with a lecherous tone to her voice, "Now, Jen, tell me about your group experience."

Jennifer actually blushed a little and gave me a shy grin. I nodded to let her know I had great empathy for her situation and feelings. She started, "Brad and I have been friends with Beth and Doug for over a year. They lived next door and had become our alter egos. Increasingly we kept finding we could share everything with them."

She looked at us, wondering if she should go on. Tiffany and I nodded encouragingly to her.

"Anyway, one night, they were over, and we were going to watch a movie we'd rented. For some reason, I felt mischievous, so I went and sat with Doug. Beth held her arms up, and Brad fell into them. The lights were low, and soon we were hugging and kissing with our new partners as the movie played. The hugging and kissing became feeling and smoothing, and then our hands were under each other's clothing. Then clothing started to come off, and then we made love to each other's mate right in the same room."

"Was it nice," Tiffany asked her sister.

"Oh, it was beautiful. We were all together and naked, enjoying the sight and feel of each other's bodies. I never

wanted the feeling to stop, but I also wanted Brad to be happy, and I wanted to love him too. We all talked about what we were feeling and how we felt about each other. We talked until two in the morning and then made love with our new partners again, then we all slept in our big bed." "Did things look different in the morning?" I asked.

"I woke up in the morning being held and cuddled by Brad. He whispered in my ear that he loved me, and it was one of those times when you know that love can move mountains. We hugged and kissed and then started to make love again, right next to Beth and Doug. They woke up and watched us, then they made love as we watched," Jennifer continued, "After we cleaned up a bit, we all went down and made breakfast. I can still remember that none of us got dressed; we were all naked. It had been a short night. We all continued talking about what we'd done and how we felt about each other. We realized we liked each other a lot and that the sex was really a confirmation of how we felt about each other. It wasn't just lust. There was a lot of love there too. We made love again after breakfast too,

and we've been an event ever since, and that was over a year ago."

Another long silence ensured, then the sisters turned to me, and Tiffany said, "You haven't told us about your threesome."

Chapter Nine

I laughed at how off guard I'd been for her question, visualizing the scene of the foursome as she'd described the details. The sisters looked puzzled, but I felt I should share this part of myself with them.

I started, "My story happened two boyfriends ago. This guy thought that having sex with two girls was great, and two girls having sex was great. He was never into being with a guy, but I found later that he didn't mind being in the same room when the guy was with me. We were right out of college, and Nate and I were in our early twenties and as horny as rabbits all the time. I gather you men have been through that stage too, or maybe you're still in it?"

Both heads nodded enthusiastically.

"So one night, one of Nate's friends was over at our apartment watching a baseball game on TV, a guy named Alan. It's hot, we don't have air conditioning, and I'm running around our apartment in just a tank top and panties. Nate gets horny watching me and gets up and puts the make on me, running his hands up under my top and fingering my slit. I look, and Alan is watching us and rubbing his shorts right where his cock is, and the bulge is evident. We're turning him on."

I paused, and both sisters leaned in. Jennifer said in an urgent voice, "Go on!"

"I felt like being an exhibitionist suddenly, so I pulled my top off completely. As you can see, there's more than a handful, so I had plenty to put on display. Nate takes it in stride and starts to suck on my breast as I'm trying to yank his shorts down. I get Nate's penis out to work it and then see that Alan is masturbating as he watches us. Next, I knew Nate had two fingers buried in me."

"Without even asking Nate, I just gestured Alan over. A split second later, I had another naked guy sucking my breasts, and I was in heaven. As they sucked on me, I ended up holding two stiff cocks in my hand."

"Someone pulled off my undies, and then I had lots of fingers inside me, and I got felt and licked all over. I must have cum a dozen times before the three of us ended on our bed. I can still remember I fucked Nate, then Alan, then Nate, then Alan. We went on for a long time, like two days taking short breaks for food and a little sleep."

"A onetime thing?" Tiffany asked.

"I thought so that night, but we got together about ten times overall. Alan was okay, and I didn't mind fucking him; he had size working to his advantage too. When I really liked Nate, so long as he was okay with what was going on, I was too. Nate and I then started to have relationship problems and ultimately broke up. We had sex after we broke up and stopped living together; we just knew there was no relationship there. Alan joined us several times after we broke up. It was all lust by then, just the three of us satisfying our carnal urges, and we had a lot of them stored up. Every time we got together, we fucked all weekend, just like our first time together."

I paused and looked at Tiffany and Jennifer. They were both on the verge of drooling at my recounting. I added, "So that's my story, and I'm stickin' to it." I'm never seeing these people again. Being honest is better than having to remember a lie.

"Hot!" said Tiffany.

Jennifer asked, "Does Ben know?"

"Not yet," I told her. "How would you go about telling someone something like that, I mean to your relatively new boyfriend? 'Oh, by the way, Ben, did I ever tell you about all the times I fucked two men until they ran out of cum?' There just never seems to be a good time." I grinned at the sisters. As Ben's 'temporary girlfriend,' I had to remember to be vague about how long we'd known each other.

Tiffany offered, "Well, you could get him involved in a threesome, and then it just wouldn't be anything worth mentioning." About that time, we heard a car in the driveway honking its horn.

"Victor and everyone," Tiffany screamed and hopped off the bed.

Tiffany and Jennifer ran out of the bedroom barefoot but wearing their final choices for cocktail dresses. They raced down the stairs to greet the newcomers. I followed at a more sedate pace to allow them time to welcome their family members.

The large home's foyer was a beehive of activity as people carried in luggage and the greeting process took place. I met Victor, the fourth member of Ben's family, his wife Katie, and Jennifer's husband, Brad.

Ben whispered that he really liked my LDB, and I told him I still needed to do makeup and other feminine things to get ready.

WEEKEND WITH AVERY

Tiffany announced that we'd all be leaving for the dinner in thirty minutes. There was a mad dash to change from work or travel clothes to our evening dress—those of us that had already started dressing, a rush to finish with makeup and shoes.

The Hotel Jerome hosted the rehearsal and dinner. I met about fifty other family members and their spouses, including Marc, Tiffany's fiancé, and Melissa, the other member of their threesome.

I tried to figure out if Marc and Melissa had that 'just fucked' look and finally decided they did. I whispered to Ben that I thought they both had that look and that I wanted to look that way too, and he told me to keep quiet. I even suggested we could go use a stall in the ladies' restroom or the coatroom. He was tempted but didn't succumb.

The other fifty people I met put my ability to remember names to a test. I thought I'd done pretty well when I could go around the large table and knew everyone's first name at least as well as their relation to the two families at the wedding.

I got to sit next to Melissa at dinner, and the two of us bonded very quickly. A pretty dishwater blond with a bubbly personality, Melissa's intelligence came through as she talked authoritatively about a wide range of subjects. Melissa turned out to be a lawyer for one of the top firms in Denver. As we got to know each other, I could feel our chemistry grow; we both promised we'd Skype or e-mail each other on one subject or another.

Ben sat next to me, and we also chatted. I got him involved in some of the conversations with Melissa. While they knew of each other, neither had met until that night.

Beyond Ben sat Tiffany and then Marc, her betrothed.

I went to the restroom and came back to this woman sitting in my seat. I hadn't been introduced to her yet. She looked older, like in her late forties. I watched her run her hand up to Ben's arm, then drape a hand around his shoulders as the two of them talked or as she shared an idea with Melissa.

A few minutes later, I watched her lean in front of Ben, one hand firmly on his thigh very close to 'ground zero.' Ben's eyes got huge, and there was no doubt of his hyperawareness of this her hand.

Ben looked at me, apparently for guidance. I acknowledged his look at me and then at the woman's hand in his lap. I walked to the woman and said. "Can I have my sit back?" She gave me a dirty look and got up and left. My reaction was to laugh. I leaned into Ben and said, "Enjoy life as it comes. You forgot to tell me about that woman." I chuckled to myself.

I planted my hand on Ben's thigh and rubbed right up to 'ground zero.' Now Ben's eyes got huge.

I asked, "Are you sure you wouldn't like to go into the coatroom?"

He looked at me and pondered the idea again. He leaned to me, and we kissed rather tenderly.

"You know this boyfriend-girlfriend thing is much, much better than I thought it would be. When I suggested that you be my 'temporary girlfriend,' I had no idea we'd be where we are now that I'd be where I am now." He kissed me again.

I smiled and decided I'd be a little coy. Ben's remark was vague, perhaps on purpose, and I knew that later I'd want some further clarification. "Changing the subject of that woman, that's fine. I'll find out later."

After the main course at dinner, Tiffany and Marc thanked everyone for coming and helping them become the people they were and assisting them in meeting and promoting their relationship. Everyone applauded.

Tiffany asked everyone that every other person at the table moved two slots to their left to meet and talk with new people for our special dessert and coffee. Half the table arose and started to mill around, mostly to their left.

I could see that woman was sitting next to Ben as the long table rearranged itself. I quickly whispered to her, "Why are you going after my boyfriend?"

I grinned at her as she digested my comment. Then I got a broad smile from her as she sat down in the seat that had been mine. "Because I can, and you can't do anything about it," she said.

I moved two slots to my left and sat with Marc on my right and Victor, Ben's brother, on my left. We broke into the conversation, and I got to know the two of them well over the intermission between dinner and dessert and then over a generous serving of Banana Foster that was Tiff's favorite. I knew I'd have to start working out after this weekend.

It might have been the flow of wine or the liqueur in the dessert that provoked my devilish nature. As Victor got into a discussion away from me, I decided to ask Marc questions about this woman. "Who's the woman next to Ben," I asked.

"That's Paula, she Tiff's mom's friend, and personal assistant. Since their parents have passed away, she helped the family. She always had a thing for Ben. I think she six years older than him. I know she has been married twice and now she's free again. I think she always wanted to be part of the family." Marc said.

"I better go save my boyfriend then," I said, walking over to Ben. I started to look deep into Ben's eyes, try to see if he understood why I touched his neck. I ran my hand up to his thigh as I leaned across to say something to Marc.

I could tell my advances on Ben were modestly successful. When Ben's hands started to wander around my body too, nothing too out of place, just a touch or smooth, supposedly to get my attention. Soon he duplicated many of my moves prompting me to raise the ante even further.

As the dinner started to break up, Marc said to me, "I am so glad you came to our wedding. You are fun and sexy and a delight to have here. Ben is a lucky man."

I leaned in and pecked a kiss on his cheek. "Thank you." I lowered my voice to a whisper, "You are a lucky man. Tiffany and Melissa are both sweethearts. I hope all our paths cross again and frequently after this weekend."

Marc looked surprised that I knew their secret. He just nodded to me as Ben came to my side. We chatted about the schedule for the wedding day, and they were off.

Ben drove me, Tiffany, Jennifer, Brad, Victor, and Katie (Victor's wife) back to Eagle Pines in a large car that the family left at the house. We were a lively group in the car, yet everyone said, 'good night' and headed off to their own rooms at home.

Ben pulled me into the living room where the remains of the pre-dinner fire still warmed the hearth. He put another couple of logs from the big log crib on the embers, and in a couple of moments, they burst into flame. He finally stood and turned to me.

I held my arms open to him. Ben closed the short space between us, and we hugged and kissed with a severe sexual intent for the first time since our passionate mile high encounter at 40,000-feet in Ben's corporate jet.

"So is the reason you brought me here was to stay away from Paula," I whispered in his ear.

"No, more my family having you here, it's a bonus to keep me always from Paula," Ben said. Well, she's not the problem that Mr. Grey had. She is a piece of work from all I see.

I felt Ben's strong hands find the zipper to my dress and shivered slightly as he toyed with the little pull and then slowly pulled the little tab all the way down to my rear. I reached up and started to undo the buttons on his shirt. My shawl and his sport coat disappeared, then seconds later, he helped me step out of my dress.

I pulled Ben's shirt off of him, revealing his muscular chest. As we kissed again, his tongue pushing into my willing mouth, he used one hand to unsnap the clasp on my black lace brassiere. I shrugged the frilly bra down my arms and tossed it in a pile with our clothes.

"I assume it's okay if we get caught making love here?" I gestured to the sofa with a silly grin.

"Of course. It'll remove all doubt that I really have a girlfriend," Ben smiled.

"A temporary girlfriend," I said with a hint of sarcasm. He didn't reply; his thoughts had moved on elsewhere. I think Ben wants to be in the imagination world, and I know after this weekend I'll be home on Tuesday crying because I will miss him. I need to be in the moment for now and take a line from Gone with the Wind. I'll think about it tomorrow.

I undid his belt and unzipped his slacks. He kicked off his loafers and stepped out of his pants. I pulled his briefs down to reveal his rising manhood. Ben looked down at me, clearly wondering what I was going to do.

I looked up into his eyes as I took his penis in both of my hands and slowly moved my hands, alternately down his cock, pulling as his engorged rod lengthened. Ben ran his fingers through my hair.

I pulled his cock into my mouth, initially licking around the mushroomed head and then capturing just the helmet of his rod in my mouth. I rapidly turned my head back and forth over the shaft holding only that top in my mouth and sucking. I heard a loud moan from my man.

I liked the heft of Ben's rod. It felt so natural to pull the entire shaft into my mouth and start bobbing up and down on the stiff shaft. I remembered some earlier lessons from years prior and took all of the swelling cock down my throat within a couple of tries. I paused, rotated my head too, and fro around his cock when the shaft was all the way into me. Ben moaned almost continuously and reminded me how wonderful I am.

"You've got to stop, stop now. I want to cum inside you, make love to you," he said in a gasp.

I slowly extracted Ben from my mouth, a long tendril of precum and saliva arching between us as we separated. I captured it with the fingers of my right hand and licked it back into my mouth.

"Yummmm," I hummed as I looked up at him. "You taste so good, but I bet all your temporary girlfriends tell you that."

"No one's ever done what you just did to me." He studied me a moment and tossed in, "There are no other temporary girlfriends, never have been."

He pulled me up, and we kissed again. Much to my surprise, he seemed more than comfortable French kissing me even after my sloppy oral lovemaking to him. The thought that no one did that to him made me happy because I was the first.

Then Ben knelt before me and pulled my black bikinis off of me. I stepped out of them as he ran his hands up and down my legs.

"Come over to the sofa, Avery."

I moved with him to the long couch now bathed in the flickering light of the fire. He hugged me again, then lowered me to the sofa, and then knelt in front of me, spreading my knees and pulling me forward to the edge of the cushions.

Ben blew on my pussy. Somehow, he knew my temperature in that region was spiking. I groaned at his forced draft.

"Your pussy is beautiful. I love this," Ben whispered.

His tongue then licked from one end of my slit to the other. Now I really groaned, then checked my volume lest I arouse one of the other household members.

"Oh, Ben."

Ben started to fuck me with his tongue, and what a talented tongue it was. Just like a small cock, he thrust his curled tongue in and out of my pussy capturing and licking my increased fluids as he did.

"You taste so good."

Fingers were added, and now I really swept into orbit. Ben instincts in no time had me writhing all over the sofa.

"Oh shit. Oh, Ben. Oh, fuck, you're gonna make me cum. Oh, don't you dare stop? Oh, what you're doing to me feels so good.

Don't ever stop. Oooooooooooh!" I came.

I know I shut my eyes, but I saw stars and fireworks as my climax swept over me. When I opened my eyes, Ben had moved so he could hold me and kiss me. I liked this boyfriend thing.

"Ben, make love to me. Fuck me. Now. Here."

He didn't need a second invitation. He rose in front of me and pulled me to the edge of the sofa again, this time carefully aiming his erect rod into me.

I had emitted so much lubricant, and with Ben's saliva adding to the fluids, he sunk in without either of us using our hands for guidance. He plunged deep in on his first stroke, and I know I moaned loudly again.

"I've wanted to do this all night with you," he told me.

I couldn't resist my next comment; "Are you sure you wouldn't have wanted to do something with Paula? She seemed to like physical contact with you tonight."

Ben looked at me, surprised. "I thought I was the only one that noticed that," he said.

"Paula, all hot for you, Ben, just the way I am. If you shut your eyes, you can fuck her," I said. I looked, and indeed Ben had closed his eyes. I felt a little extra jab as he thrust into me.

Ben moaned barely under his breath, and his thrusting pace changed again.

As I elevated my cunt to meet his thrusts, I paused again, then shifted characters.

"Or maybe Paula and I would have pulled you into the coatroom, and you could have fucked the two of us. Can you imagine that?"

As Ben pumped into me, I glanced up at the balcony surrounding the living room. Paula in the shadows, naked in the dim dancing light from the fire. Did she go to Ben's room and not find him there? Fantasy might be acceptable, but I don't think he ever slept with Paula. Thus, instead, I revisited the little scenarios I had been painting for him, adding detail.

I whispered quietly enough so the person on the balcony could not hear, "Imagine you've got your cock buried in Paula. You'd like that, wouldn't you? You've wanted to house sex with her for years, haven't you?"

Ben nodded but kept his eyes closed as he thrust into me.

"What would you tell her?"

He spoke aloud, and I knew she could hear him. "I'd tell her how I love her once, but after our first time together, after my parents died. I'd pound into her like this," Ben said as he pulled almost all the way out of me and then thrust back into me in a long, powerful stroke. I moaned.

"And like this," he went on and repeated the process of stroking into my body.

I looked and could see Paula and her hand between her legs. "Come back to me, Ben. Make love to me. I'm about to cum. Cum in me. Cum in me. Open your eyes, so I know you are with me."

With that, I locked my legs behind Ben and pulled him into me, urging him at a rapid pace, encouraging his deep drives.

Our eyes locked on one another's, and he pounded into me. Then suddenly, we both crested.

I shrieked, "Oh fuck, you've made me cum again." Ben moaned a long groan of love and contentment.

The balcony was silent, but I could see Paula as her orgasm swept over her. Ben nuzzled into me and said, "Avery, you are so special. You're unbelievable." We kissed.

When I looked again, Paula had disappeared from her viewpoint.

Ben said, "You are something. I couldn't imagine a more seductive person in my life than you just were. Where did you learn to do that, to say things like that?"

"Romance novels that I've read that are so hot, I wanted to try it with someone. You bring out the best in me," I said. "Besides, I've been thinking about little else but sex for the past twentyfour hours. Even when I talked to your sisters this afternoon." I paused and added, "Especially when I talked to your sisters this afternoon."

"Why do you say that?" Ben asked as he leaned in and kissed my eyelids and cheeks.

"We got to telling stories about ourselves this afternoon, sex stories. There's one, in particular, you should know about right now. Tiffany asked that I tell you, but you can't tell anyone, including Victor, because only a few people know."

Ben looked at me in anticipation of hearing a sexy story. I could even feel his penis twitch in my vagina and took that sign as an expression of interest.

"You know that Tiffany and Marc live together and have for a couple of years?" I asked.

"Sure," Ben said, "that's not been a secret."

"Well, Melissa also lives with them; they're really a throuples, no a couple."

Ben twitched again inside me. He said, "Wow! Now that's news. Full participation all around?"

"Oh, yes," I said. "So much so that Tiffany made sure Melissa and Marc had connecting rooms at the Lodge so the two of them could be together while she's here. Remember, I figured out they'd have sex just before the dinner well, it was with each other! Tiffany is bisexual, at least as far as Melissa. And, if you'd turned around and looked up into the balcony five minutes ago while we were fucking you would have seen Paula playing with herself while she watched us."

Ben rolled to the sofa beside me. His cock was still somewhat rigid despite our lovemaking only moments before.

"One more thing," I said as I leaned in and kissed him, "Jennifer and Brad have a relationship with another couple they live near. They share and get together for intimate games and extend their relationship a couple of times a week. Based on the way they're talking, and what I figured out tonight, I bet that circle will widen to include Tiffany, Marc, and Melissa, all seven of them."

"You know that makes me harden just to think of all the possibilities," Ben said.

"You don't mind girl-girl things?" I asked.

"You're kidding right, that's every guy's dream come true," he said. "Right at this second, they're almost the hottest thing I can imagine next to making love with you again."

I shifted off the sofa and bent down next to Ben's waist. Just before I inhaled his cock again, I said, "Then let's not let this opportunity and this nice fire go to waste." I licked at his penis like a sucker, sucking his entire length into my mouth and enjoying the evident mix of our body fluids.

A few minutes later, I mounted him, and we each had another orgasm. Ben became more rigid and more swollen than I'd known him to be, and soon he was delivering his extra pleasure to me too.

After we recuperated, we collected our clothes and walked up the stairs naked to our bedroom suite. I didn't see Paula again that night, but I swore I heard muffled moans from behind one of the bedroom doors. Someone else was having sex tonight.

Chapter Ten

When I woke the next morning, Ben's body pressed against mine in a tight spoon. I could feel his inflating cock and then knew for sure that he was awake. I felt him use one hand to position his rod at the entrance to my pussy.

I raised a leg to give him full access. I'd retained most of the fluids from our play the night before, and immediate lubrication was not an issue. Soon Ben was penetrating in and out of my body. A girl could get used to this kind of treatment.

After our orgasms had passed and we lay there panting, I rolled into Ben's arms so we could kiss. The fluids from our fuck trickled across my leg, yet I thought it kind of sexy, so I ignored the tracks.

We kissed and hugged for quite a while, cooing and smoothing each other. I love to have my breasts stroked, particularly after making love, and that morning was no exception. "You were really turned on last night. I like you like that," I said.

"Thanks to you," Ben said.

"So why are you not with Paula? She really wants you?" I asked.

"Paula's only good trait is lying and using people," Ben stated. "She can't be that bad? Your sister loves her if she here," "Hell, yes she is. My sisters know it too," he said with a grin. "I may have to rethink my priorities. Having you as a temporary girlfriend has sure opened my eyes to what I've been missing in my life."

I told him, "My grandma told me to keep a man in my life is to keep him satisfied in bed and feed him well. But what I've found that you need an inner balance between food, love, the need to be needed, and trust. If you one do one disregarded the others, you will have no real life. Everyone needs a sense of achievement and happiness."

"You're profound, too," Ben told me as he kissed my nose. "Those thoughts nicely summarize what I've been rolling around in my head since we really met and started talking with each other. I'm ready to change to expand my purview of life beyond the foundation."

"What about your family?" I asked, purposefully leaving the full scope of the question unstated.

"I already love them. I need to spend more time with them. Since college, I've neglected them although they've turned out well and have thriving careers."

Now I kissed Ben on the nose and then ran my tongue down his neck.

"I'm happy, thrilled if you are. If we can play and enjoy ourselves together, I will savor every moment. Besides, we are enjoying being a couple this weekend. Even if I have to deal with Paula and her hands."

"You're jealous?" he asked.

"No, not a bit. You're my pretend boyfriend, and I have no right to be jealous," I started. "If I really like someone like you,

I want to see you happy, fulfilled, stretching your limits, and watch your growth. If I put a lid on all the interactions with other people, I stifle you, and soon you'll resent me and what I represent because you'll feel that loss too." I kissed him on his nose and added, "Besides, the idea of you having sex with someone else with me turns me on."

"What would you be doing while I was making love to someone else?" Ben asked.

"Perhaps joining in some way was dedicated to my pleasure."

Ben thought a long time again as he kissed my left breast. He said, "You know that is erotic to think about. One way I could feel jealous that it's not me making love to you, and the other is I'm turned on and glad you are being pleasured by someone in a way that turns you on."

"I want my lover to know I'll accept what they want to do. As long as we talk about it and agree," I said.

We hugged and kissed some more, and then there was a banging on the door to our bedroom.

Ben flipped the sheet up over us and yelled, "Come in!"

Jennifer and Tiffany came bounding into the room like two *Tigger*'s from *Winnie the Pooh*. They were full of energy and excited beyond belief. Both were wearing pajamas that had bride and bride-maid on them.

"Were you two screwing?" Tiffany asked devilishly.

"Finished fifteen minutes ago," I responded with a smirk.

"Just laying here talking about love, sex, and other things like that."

Jennifer looked at me and said, "We're going to the spa in town for the 'works,' and you're invited to my treat. Please come. We really want you with us. Paula and Crystal, the other two bridesmaids, are coming too."

"Paula's going? I don't know if I want Avery going?" Ben said.

"I'm in," I yelled. I tossed back the covers and got out of bed nude. Ben still had his midriff covered. The sisters watched me prance naked across the room towards the bathroom. "Just let me take a quick shower, and I'll be ready."

"I don't like this. I want to keep Avery, and Paula has a way of making them leave," I heard Ben say. Interesting, I thought.

My shower probably lasted three minutes. The 'works' at most spas would finish everything else I might have thought about and then some. I wrapped a towel around me and walked back into the bedroom.

He was still covered in bed, and Tiffany and Jennifer told him that everything would be fine. "I will be safe, and no one is going to make me not want you, even Paula."

The girls said we had thirty minutes and walked out of the room. I pulled a top from my suitcase and slipped it over my head, adjusting the bright colored garment as it reached my waist. I'd already decided to skip the bra. I looked at Ben, "You really need to relax, Ben. No woman is going to take me away from you no matter what she says. Only you can do that."

Ben grinned and nodded. I leaned in and kissed him. He reached up under my top and rubbed my breasts, bringing the nipples back to an erect state. I batted his hand away.

I pulled the cover back and lowered my head to his somewhat flatted cock. I sucked the entire sausage into my mouth and used my tongue and cheeks to massage him. When I could feel some blood surge back, and I pulled off of him.

"Hold that thought until later." I turned and stepped into some slacks and put on some flats from my suitcase. I blew Ben a kiss and headed downstairs to meet the others and head for the spa.

Men don't appreciate the near orgasmic delight that a spa provides a woman. There were six of us from the wedding party:

Tiffany, Jennifer, Melissa, Paula, Crystal, and me. We did get the works.

At one point in the four hours, I sat nude in the sauna when Tiffany came in and joined me, quickly shedding her towel.

"Oh, hey," I said, "I haven't told you. I talked to Ben last night and this morning. I told him about you, Melissa and Marc."

"How'd he take it," she asked with a hopeful tone to her voice.

"He seemed receptive to it. Ben said, if your happy, he's happy for you." I grinned at her but didn't say a word.

She jumped up and down with glee, "Oh, goody. Now I can be honest around Ben" After coming back down, she asked.

"When are you flying back to Seattle?"

"Late Monday, I guess," I said. "Ben thought there might be enough snow up here to ski, but most of it's gone, so skiing is out."

"How'd you like to fly us to Puerto Vallarta tomorrow morning and stay until late Monday, or even later in the week if you can? We can get to know each other really well." Tiffany's flying into my arms.

"I like the way you think," I told Tiff. "Are you sure you want the two of us horning in on your honeymoon?"

"Oh, most definitely. Marc and Melissa would be delighted too," Tiff said.

The door to the sauna opened, and Melissa came in closely followed by Jennifer. They assessed our naked bodies and immediately dropped the towels they came wrapped in.

Melissa's body was magnificent. She had full round breasts that I assumed were also the result of implants. She carried them well. She was tanned all over except for a small patch of whiter skin where a tiny bikini must have shaded her skin. Her long hair had been piled atop her head and pinned in place with a couple of loose strands hanging down beside her pretty face.

Jennifer and Tiffany shared nice bodies too. Both women had long slender legs and hips, flat stomachs, and even the hint of abs that showed they worked out frequently. They were both probably C-cups like me, but on their slenderer bodies, their breasts looked more inviting. Long necks and pretty faces led up to their brunette hair. Both had functional haircuts, no doubt to make life more comfortable in the morning when they got ready for work.

"Avery's going to try to get Ben to fly us to Puerto Vallarta tomorrow," Tiffany told Melissa and Jennifer. "If possible, they'll join us for a day or so." She gave Melissa a lecherous grin. "We can join the mile-high club!"

The door opened, and Paula walked in and dropped her towel next. I could feel my temperature rise. Why did I want to hit her? "Paula, did you enjoy the show last night," I asked.

"I would rate it as a five because Ben can do so much better than that," Paula said. Both Tiffany's and Jennifer's mouths dropped.

"That's not what he told me after I told him you were watching us. Ben said that you were always better at watching than doing."

"You have the game, girl," Tiffany said.

"I can see why my brother is dating you," Jennifer said.

"Well, when he's done with his little whore of many, he will be coming for me. You see, I'm family, and he comes to me when he's done with the likes of you," Paula said, standing up.

I stood up when the door opened, and one of the spa attendants stuck her head in the door and said in a cheery voice, "Okay, Avery, you're about done. Time to come out now, shower, manicure, pedicure, and then we'll start doing your hair for the wedding."

The door shut. I grabbed my towel and wrapped it around me. Tiffany stood and hugged me again, and so did her sister, saying we will take care of this.

"Later," Tiffany said.

"Later," I said. I rewrapped my towel around my naked body and left the hot room.

Two hours later, Tiffany, Jennifer, Melissa, and I rode back to the Eagle Pines, the large family home. I have to say, except for our casual clothes, we were four of the most beautiful women in the world. Our conversation revolved around details about the wedding and the reception, both of which were to be held at the Elkhorn Lodge in Aspen's older downtown area.

Tiffany told me she had a surprise for me when we got back to the lodge. I love surprises.

This surprise almost knocked me over. As we reached Eagles and went upstairs, Tiffany led me to her bedroom and, just as we got to the door, said to me, "I want you to be in my wedding.".

Chapter Eleven

"I want you to be a bridesmaid." She held my hand. "I'll make sure you get Ben."

I stopped cold in my tracks. "But … why … how …?" I stammered and blubbered as tears of joy came to my eyes. "I'm not ready, I just …" A speechless state overtook me as I looked through my blurred eyes at her.

"Come," she said. She opened the door to her room, and there on the bed was her wedding dress and another bridesmaid dress. "This should fit you unless I am a terrible judge of what size you are. Come on, let's get dressed."

I cried aloud as the two of us hugged. I felt such love from her, and I hope she could feel how I felt about her.

"Who was Ben's bridesmaid in the lineup?" I asked.

"Paula, but after today we thought it be better if you were with Ben," Tiffany said.

Jennifer and Melissa had gone to Jennifer's room to change.

I stripped back down to my thong and reached the same stage of undress as Tiffany did.

"I sure hope that brother of mine brings you to Mexico. We both like you, and I hope my brother doesn't let you go." Tiffany said. "Let's get dressed, or we won't be ready on time."

I was ready in fifteen minutes, and that even included helping Tiffany get into most of her wedding dress, a simple floorlength white satin strapless sheath. She looked beautiful in it, and I started to tear up all over again.

The bridesmaid dress was a lovely spaghetti-strapped mango colored floor-length sheath. A slit up the side to midthigh allowed a full stride and revealed a lot of legs. The bodice left me with an impressive display of cleavage. We both laughed when I commented on how the dress invited Ben to put his hand down my front and fondle my breasts.

Tiffany added that Marc or Brad might also like to explore that geography and part of the southern hemisphere.

Jennifer and Melissa joined us, dressed just like I was. We were four beautiful women, and I knew that Paula and Crystal would be just as pretty. This was going to be a gorgeous wedding.

I lovingly hugged Tiffany. "Thank you so much for inviting me to be at your wedding. I feel so swept up in your family and ... well, I'm falling in love with all of you so fast." We hugged, and I let her go. We both smiled warmly at each other.

Ben knocked on the door and yelled in, "Limousines are here. Time to go, ladies. Your escorts are all gathered in the hall. Well, most of them are."

I opened the door. Ben was impressive in his tuxedo. I instantly thought he could have stepped out of a *James Bond* movie. A scene in some grand casino in Monte Carlo where he's just leaving and about to get into his million-dollar Aston Martin.

Ben looked deep into my eyes and said, "You are beautiful. You were beautiful before you went out this morning, and now you are even more beautiful if that's possible. You take my breath away."

I flowed into his arms, and we carefully hugged so my repaired makeup didn't smudge onto his tux. We pecked at each other's lips.

Brad came into the room also looking dashing. He and Jennifer kissed and hugged. The men all fawned appropriately over Tiffany, kissing her and telling her how beautiful the bride looked.

Our whole entourage headed downstairs and out the front door into the waiting stretch limousine. Fifteen minutes later, we pulled up in front of the Elkhorn Lodge, the wedding and reception site.

The wedding consisted of a circle of the bridesmaids and groomsmen surrounding the New Age minister, Marc, and Tiffany. All the guests stood in concentric semi-circles behind them. Everyone held hands as a symbol of unity, love, and support for the couple and each other. As the simple ceremony ended, the minister had us all hug one another and spread the attendees' warmth and love. The scene could have come out of a movie. Everyone looked so happy.

At the reception, Ben and I sat at one of the round tables in the great hall with six other people. We all introduced ourselves and exchanged pleasantries as the appetizers were served. Finally, I had an opportunity to tell Ben about the spa conversation and ask him about flying us all to Puerto Vallarta.

He shot me a wide grin and said, "What a great idea." He leaned in and whispered to me, "I want to make love to you on the beach."

I whispered back, "You can make love to me on the beach if you play your cards right." I ran my fingers up his thigh, stopping just short of his crotch. I could watch his eyes enlarge the closer I got to ground zero.

"Sounds like a plan," Ben said back to me, "but just so you know, you are my first priority." I could tell by the look on his face that he was serious.

During dinner, the two of us steered our conversation to more mundane things about our lives that we both wanted to know. We shared our childhoods with each other: talking about siblings, early schooling, parents, and other factors influential on our views of the world, things we hadn't gotten to as he was preparing me for this trip as his 'temporary girlfriend.'

Often, we'd veer off our learning about each other to allow conversation with someone else at the table. I'm sure the other six people, all more middle-aged couples, evaluated us as hopelessly falling in love with one another in hindsight.

After dinner, Marc and Tiffany cut a rather traditional looking wedding cake. A six-piece band then started to crank out some fantastic music that appealed to all the attendees. They had a knack for getting people involved in the dancing as individual band members wandered into the audience and pulled the wallflowers out onto the dance floor.

Ben went and had his 'mandatory' dance with Tiffany as I danced with Marc. The piece we danced to allowed us to dance close to each other.

A little later, we got a chance to dance with Jennifer and Brad.

I could also see a loving relationship with his sisters too. I hope Brad and Marc never hurt them because Ben will take them out. When the dance ended, we changed partners, and I plastered myself against Ben and let him squire me around the dance floor.

Paula went to ask Ben to dance. He didn't say no. He had danced with all the bridesmaids, so he couldn't say no to her.

"Are you okay, Avery?" Jennifer asked me while I was watching them dance.

"I feel like I shouldn't be having these feelings about Ben," I said. Tiffany must have heard what I said.

"Great," Tiffany said, "Paula has you thinking bad thoughts."

"Yes. No, I don't know. I can see why Paula doesn't want to give this family up. I like you all so much now. If Paula is right, I'll be one of many he will forget."

"Neither do we. We think you're great, and so does my brother," she said. "That's why I'm so glad you're coming to Mexico with us."

On that note, we hugged one another with great affection.

The band stopped playing about midnight, and that pretty much broke up the party. Marc and Tiffany had already slipped away back to Eagle Pines. We all laughed at the idea of them culminating their marriage; they had already lived together for two years.

We gathered another limousine full of people and headed back to the house, thanking the Lodge staff and the band for the beautiful evening they'd put on for our crowd.

As soon as we got to the Eagles Pines, Victor and Katie disappeared for the night, and right behind them, Brad and Jennifer went to bed.

We climbed up the stairs to get to our room, and Ben undressed me.

As we kissed, I caught Ben's cock between my legs and moved my hips back and forth as I squeezed him in place. He hardened further from when I'd gone to him.

"Come with me, Avery. Let's make love in our bedroom."

We broke apart, and Ben pulled me down the short corridor to our bedroom. A queen-size bed graced the room with other bedroom furniture. Ben led me to the ground and pushed me onto my back.

Then Ben's tongue, that marvelous tongue, found my slit, and in no time at all, he had me writhing and starting to cum.

He introduced me to something called the 'Hummingbird.' He made maximum mouth contact with my pussy, particularly my clit, and then started a low-frequency hum or buzz.

Ben had superb oral talents. Within sixty seconds, he demonstrated a unique facility to bring a woman to orgasm and prolong the pleasure in her body.

I shifted into a talkative mood as he worked my pussy over with his tongue, rising towards various peaks as each second went by. "Oh, fuck. Ben, you are superb. Where'd you ever learn how to do this? Oh, dear, my clit is ... right ... THERE! Oh, good, God. How'd ... Oh fuck."

In ten minutes, he brought me to two orgasms. Further, every time my body flushed, I gushed some girl juice in his face and got physically hotter. I know I was soaking the bed sheets but didn't want to stop.

I finally regained sufficient composure to ask Ben to bury his cock in my pussy. "Come to me, you wonderful man. Make love to me."

I sort of liked the way the last couple of statements sounded, almost farcical in a way.

Ben pumped into me for a few minutes then literally picked me up without 'breaking lock' with me. He spun me around the room as I held on to him – arms around his neck; legs around his waist; his cock buried in my cunt. I couldn't believe he could do that.

After he bounced me around a little on his cock, he lay down on the bed with me atop him. In this position, he could be more relaxed and fondle, lick and suck on my breasts.

I told Ben as I got nearer and nearer to my third orgasm of the hour. He was almost there too.

"Fill me with your cum," I said.

I allowed myself to crest as well, just as I felt the first of Ben's juices surge into my vagina. He surged ... and surged ... and surged.

We fell asleep after the night before, and the night before that, we were both tired. You can't have sex every night and get up early without it hitting you.

Chapter Twelve

We woke to "Breakfast in fifteen minutes," Tiffany yelled.

"I thought she would be sleeping in," I said.

"She's excited to start her honeymoon," Ben replied in midyawn. He then looked at me. "Time for a quickie?"

I nodded. Ben proved that he couldn't be in the presence of a naked woman without developing a severe hard-on. I pulled Ben over me, and he sank into me. "I wanted to get to Mexico fast too, but not before we finished our quickie," I whispered.

As quickies go, this proved to be arousing and very satisfying. We were learning each other's buttons and how to bring pleasure to one another in short order. We did. Ben did. I did. Wow!

After our showers and quickly repacking our clothes, we went downstairs. Ben grabbed a glass of orange juice and disappeared into the den to do the flight planning for our trip to Puerto Vallarta.

He rejoined Marc, Tiffany, Melissa, and me as we finished some scrambled eggs Tiffany had whipped up. Ben wolfed down a helping as he told us about the flight details.

He said, "The distance from here to Puerto Vallarta is 1,285 miles or 1,115 nautical miles. We'll travel about 420 knots, so the trip down will take about three hours, including climb out and descent. The weather is superb over the entire route, and we might get a tailwind part of the way. They expect the temperatures to be in the mid-eighties by noon, and the water temperature is just over eighty. Light breezes. Sounds pretty perfect to me."

We snuck out of the house without waking the others. Tiffany left a note on behalf of all of us.

Half an hour later, we were at the Aspen, Colorado airport. Twenty minutes later, the jet lifted off the runway into the bright morning skies over Colorado. Twenty minutes after that, we were near altitude and on our flight plan route to PVR.

Ben had me sit as co-pilot again.

Our morning sexual romp had left me satisfied for the time being, so I wasn't about to jump Ben's bones at 40,000 feet. Our three passengers, however, decided they'd join the Mile-High Club. I peeked back into the cabin after we got to altitude. Saw Marc lying around on one of the leather seats with a 'died and gone to heaven' look on his face as Melissa and Tiffany took turns riding his cock. All three were nude. I pulled the curtain to give them the privacy that they didn't seem to need but to remove my own temptation to join them.

"They're all going to be on the Mile-high club after this flight," I said.

"Good for them," Ben said.

I asked Ben to start giving me a lesson about the airplane and its instrumentation. I allowed that to consume me despite the moans and shrieks from the passenger compartment. Ben actually let me make some gentle S-turns and get a feel for the controls of the jet. By the time we landed, I felt more comfortable with the plane, even going so far as to consider getting a pilot's license. He explained the process to me.

We cleared customs, got a rental car and drove into the old part of the town, and had lunch at a place Katie had recommended. Her recommendation turned out to be excellent, and we got a wonderful meal and good service.

After lunch, I hadn't brought a bathing suit, so we stopped in a tourist shop and bought a bikini that I thought might have arousal powers to it.

Tiffany and Marc had rented a villa for the week that turned out to be about fifteen minutes north of the airport on the Bay of Banderas, a small open bay into the Pacific Ocean.

The home was impressive, sitting on a cliff overlooking the Pacific and the Bay, with large rooms that opened onto a flagstone deck, beach, and pool. Dense foliage and surrounding the area gave security. The wall ensured privacy from neighbors, plus we were far enough away from the usual tourist hotels that even the pristine beach didn't have casual walkers on it.

After we'd all walked around the house, Tiffany announced that it was beach time. In minutes Melissa, Tiffany, and I ran from the house down to the beach in our bikinis, the men following at a slower pace. As I paused before splashing into the warm water, I could look both ways along the beach and only see about a half dozen people, most far down the beach towards the airport. I could see no one in the other direction.

Marvelous.

My new white and yellow bikini became almost transparent when it got wet, something I didn't know until Ben came to me and kissed me, running his tongue down to my breasts. "You're on display, Love," he said, "if that makes any difference to you."

I looked down and saw my state; "Well, I wanted a seductive bathing suit. I guess that'll do." I grinned, knowing I never had a problem with my body, and no one else seemed to care.

We were bobbing around on our backs in the clear water. Marc had found some facemasks and snorkel tubes and gave me a set to try.

Seconds later, my eyes took in the sights under the bay's surface, including a wide variety of beautiful looking little fish and an occasional conch shell.

The five of us swam and sunned for over an hour, taking care not to burn since we'd also forgotten to bring or buy suntan lotion. After an hour, I went up to the shade of some palm trees that surrounded the pool deck, moving a lounger around so I could be in the shade. The gentle sea breeze dried me off in minutes. I lay back and was asleep in an instant.

I think I had some erotic dreams. In any case, they ended erotically as I felt my pussy flush with attention. I gradually regained consciousness.

As my eyes blinked open, I found Ben bending over me and blowing his hot breath on my bathing suit, right on the thin fabric covering my clitoris. No wonder I felt flushed and 'hot.'

I pulled him on top of me, and we went into a kiss that turned into a French kiss.

"Can we make love to each other now?" I asked with an impatient tone to my voice.

"Yes, Love. It's time," he whispered as he kissed me again.

"Let's take this inside. We don't want to shock the natives," Ben said.

Ben pulled me up from the lounger. We walked the few paces to the bedroom, entering the room directly from the patio through gossamer curtains that swayed with the sea breeze off the Bay. We pulled the suits from our bodies.

I dropped to my knees and turned Ben's hips towards me so I could have access to his cock. I pulled his rod to my mouth and started a verbal assault on his tool, holding him as the blood surged into his manhood.

When I had him rock hard, and his cock stood straight out from his body, we fell side by side.

In another second, Ben sank his entire swollen cock into my pussy, pausing at rock bottom for the two of us to savor the penetration.

"Oh, God, Fi," Ben gasped; "We should have done this after our first encounter. We wasted all this time waiting and wondering what it'd be like."

I reached up and stroked his face, "We're doing it now, and that's all that counts. Forget about lost opportunities and think of all the times we have ahead of us."

Ben kissed me deeply then rolled me onto my back. Ben reached across and stroked my cheek. "Avery, thank you. I can't make it go away other than tell you I care for you more now than ever."

Despite my curiosity about Ben's volume, I went into my heaven, closing my eyes for a minute as the pleasure surged through me. We then held each other tight, and as our climaxes waned, we kissed passionately. As the crest slid totally by, our kisses and stroking became more tender and loving.

I lifted myself up off his cock and shifted up the bed just in time as a drop of cum dripped from my vagina and spread out over Ben's pubic area and abdomen.

I waited until the drips stopped, then clasped a hand over my pussy and, with some awkward gyrations, got off the bed and walked into the adjacent bathroom. A couple of minutes later, I came back to the bedroom with a warm washcloth.

Ben hadn't touched the cum pools on his body.

Now I love cum. I like the taste, the texture, and the naughty thought of swallowing it, particularly knowing that it's something most women don't or won't do.

I draped the washcloth over the bedside table and moved between Ben's legs. I took his moist cock and cleaned him up.

The sea breeze floated into the room, making all of us perspire from our efforts. We could hear the palms swishing against each other outside the large French doors that opened onto the pool patio.

We all heard two splashes and some laughter from Marc, Tiffany, and Mellissa. They called out to us: "Come join us in the pool if you're done – it's a great way to clean up and cool off. Come on, men. Hurry before we use up all the water."

We looked at each other, and thirty seconds later, we were in the water too.

The five of us bobbed around the pool for almost an hour. The sun was low in the sky. Marc found that the house had been stocked with wine and champagne for us and brought out some liquid refreshments.

Ben and I cuddled together at one point down by one end of the pool. I told him, "You know I could be delighted with just you?"

He nodded and said, "Yes, and I hope you realize I feel the same way." He grinned and said. "That said, it had been a great weekend – far, far beyond anything I'd expected or even dreamed about when I asked you to be my temporary girlfriend."

"I like this temporary girlfriend role." I leaned in and kissed him, making sure my breasts pushed against his chest and arm.

"Well, you're very good at it," he said in a teasing voice. "We might use you again sometime."

"If this is how you use people, I could get used to it," I gestured towards the other three.

"Seriously, are you all right with me, and what happened this weekend?" Ben asked, I took Ben's face gently in one hand, turned his head to me, and kissed him. "I'm more than okay with it. I liked being your focal point this weekend, and if none of the other stuff had happened, I'd be just as happy."

I thought for a moment and asked Ben, "Are you all right with all that's happened? Did I burn any bridges here or do anything that'll put me on your shit list?"

"No, absolutely not, quite the opposite. I met you last Monday at *Starbucks,* and we introduced ourselves. A lot has happened since then. One surprise right after another; I've probably had too many surprises in too short a period."

Ben paused and looked down the pool where Marc, Melissa, and Tiffany were floating serenely on their backs. He thought a moment and added, "Your willingness to participate in my family setting became a surprise. You fit in so well with my family, and I've never had that before. Avery, you have been perfect and a joyful surprise." I got a warm smile and a hug.

We kissed and nuzzled some more. I know we both felt better having talked about the past few days as we did.

Chapter Thirteen

The sun had almost set as the five of us piled into the car and drove into the touristy part of the old town.

Much to our surprise, the city had become a beehive of activity. We found a little family restaurant with tables in a small plaza on a side street and decided to eat there. Melissa spoke Spanish and helped with the ordering; our thanks to the family that ran the restaurant and made our stay memorable.

Sunday night at the Villa proved to be interesting. Ben and I would be alone for the night, and that would be it.

Ben said, "The two of us want some alone time too. See you in the morning."

As the three of them walked from view into their bedroom. Ben and I returned to our room, kissing and smoothing one another.

"Will you make love to me on the beach? I've never done it there, and I want to with you?" I asked him.

We grabbed two towels and put on our suits, and headed to the pool. We swam for an hour. Ben led me up the pool steps, gathered a beach blanket and several beach towels from the pile on the patio, and led me down the Bay and the Pacific steps.

We picked a spot just up from the tide line. The beach was deserted, and the night was dark. A sliver of a moon had just started to appear over the eastern sky.

Ben lay back, and I sucked on his handsome cock. The two of us wanted this time alone and unrushed.

Ben hardened, and I mounted him. I rode him for a long time, alternating speeds, often rolling my hips around to give him entirely different sensations. We repositioned. Ben fucked me from behind. I liked that position, for his long cock stimulated my G-spot, and it wasn't long before I allowed myself another orgasm.

Ben ate my pussy for a while, driving me ever higher with his talented tongue and lips. I urged him back in me, and he re-entered from several different angles.

We came together, surrounded by the gentle breaking waves beside us and the panoply of stars over our heads. The experience was truly spiritual, a union of our souls and the Universe. I will dream of this night over and over again.

After our afterglow had waned, Ben picked me up and carried me up to the house. We briefly dipped in the pool to wash off the beach and our last lovemaking session, then we crashed into the night on another of the large beds locked in each other's arms.

Ben kissed me awake the next morning. I blinked awake.

"No fair," I said, "I have morning breath that would kill a dragon from the Mexican food I ate last night."

He laughed and told me not to worry but that I should get up. "There's some sort of crew in the kitchen and the aromas and making my mouth water."

"I'm supposed to make your mouth water, not food!" I told him playfully.

He retorted, "Ah, but without food, my ability to deliver pleasure to you will vanish. I'll end as nothing but a pile of famished bones."

He pulled away but grabbed my arms and gently pulled me to a vertical position. I gradually got out of bed and went to the bathroom. When I came out, I asked Ben, "What are people wearing?"

"PJ's," he replied. "It's a come as you are breakfast." He smiled lecherously at me. I floated into his arms, and we kissed, my mouth now tasting like peppermint toothpaste.

In the beautiful kitchen, Marc had mastered the coffee maker. Seemed pleased to contribute some of the dark liquid to the cups at our places around the counter. Tiffany had found fruit containers, and Melissa had found enough eggs and other fixings to wrestle up a Mexican omelet for us. All three wore PJs that said bride, bride, and Groom, and they all matched.

"You men okay with what happened last night?" Tiffany asked after we were seated and eating.

"Better than okay," I told her. "It's a night we'll never forget." I looked at Ben. "We both loved every second of it. We joined the 'Sex on the Beach Club' after you men slipped away." I grinned at Ben; he looked proud of himself.

Tiffany turned to Marc and said, "Put that on our 'to make' list." He laughed and rolled his eyes.

"What is on your list?" I asked the group rhetorically.

Melissa chimed in, "I'd like to see the market. I hear there are all sorts of crafts and artwork there. I'd also like to walk around and take pictures in the marina. Would you men like that ... or do you want to go back to your room and have something more physical?" She snickered at her last comment.

Ben answered for both of us, "We're fine physically, for now. I need to rest, and I'd like to spend a little fun time, the nonsexual kind, down here with my girlfriend. I opt for walking around the market and marina for us. I'd like to get airborne right after lunch. We'll be flying into the clock." I nodded my agreement with Melissa and Ben.

"Okay, it's decided," Melissa announced. "Of course, you two can stay here and consummate your marriage again if you want to."

Marc and Tiffany looked at each other, then laughed. Tiffany said with a tone of great reluctance, "No, we'll come to the market." She looked at Marc and added, "But we do have some serious fucking plans for later this afternoon."

An hour later, Ben and I had packed our bags and had put them in the car. The five of us drove back to the central part of the small city and played tourist for the morning. I bought some little gifts for some of my co-workers. I got a couple of things for myself in the market.

Melissa took about a thousand pictures, particularly around the marina where she had us pose against the picturesque background. She got some passersby to take group photos of the five of us, and I made her promise to email them all to me. I wondered if the images and couple of Mexican crafts I'd bought would be the only things left from this weekend.

Somehow the reality that this was my last day as a 'temporary girlfriend' had started to hit home. I had a deep feeling of nostalgia; I didn't want this time to end. I wasn't sure what Ben thought, but I wanted our newly formed relationship to continue. While he'd professed, he liked me. Ben felt I fit into his unusual family. He'd also been remarkably silent about what would happen in our lives after this weekend.

We ate lunch at a seafood restaurant that overlooked the marina. After our meal, Marc drove us out to the airport. Four of us stood and talked while Ben paid for the plane's overnight stay and fuel, checked the weather, and filed our flight plan. A U.S. customs agent stationed at the airport came and reviewed our papers and the plane, allowing our re-entry into the U.S. without needing to stop for a further customs check.

The family promises to visit each other either in Colorado or Seattle soon. We all bid each other goodbye with a hail of kisses and bear hugs. I secretly wondered if I'd see any of them again.

Ben and I climbed in the jet, folded up the stairway, and settled into the cockpit as the others walked across the tarmac to watch our takeoff.

Ben ran through several checklists and reminded me about safety exits and oxygen. He had me put my hand on the throttles as he advanced them, and the plane started to move. He showed me how to steer the plane with my feet through the rudder pedals. We taxied to the end of the runway while Ben talked to ground control and got our clearance.

Ben explained, "We're flying to Denver to refuel. I have to pick-up something there too, a family thing that Jennifer brings to the airport for me. Pull back on the throttles just a little; keep your ground speed low as you taxi. This plane builds up a lot of momentum."

I nodded my acknowledgment but over-corrected by pulling the throttles back too far. Ben's steady hand on mine quickly corrected my mistake.

Near the runway end, we stopped and ran through a couple of checklists; Ben switched the radio over to the tower frequency and informed them we were ready to take off. The crisp voice from the tower cleared us to the active runway for takeoff and told us to contact departure control on 126.25 Mhz after launch.

I would have a lot to learn if I took up flying.

We took off towards the ocean and used about 4,800 feet of runway. Ben set our climb out at about 2,000 feet per minute. We bid tower goodbye and switched to departure; they cleared us to flight level 410 and, after several minutes, had us change frequencies to Mexicali enroute center.

Ben walked me through some of the instruments again and talked me through the entire flight, relating it to his flight planning. He showed me some of the computer printouts he'd done at the Puerto Vallarta airport. He explained each one, including reading the gibberish that turned out to be terminal weather reports.

The time flew by, and soon we'd started our descent. Ben explained we were flying into the Airport, a general aviation airport fifteen miles southeast of downtown Denver. We'd refuel there, pick up the things Ben was expecting, and then fly on to Seattle.

We started our descent over New Mexico, and again, I loved flying over the mountains. Ben pointed out Pike's Peak and the Air Force Academy as we left the mountains for the foothills of the Rockies. Fifteen minutes later, our tires squealed loudly as the sleek jet set down on the tenthousand-foot-long runway. We rolled out and taxied to one of the buildings for refueling and our stop. Ben shut down the jet's engines, and suddenly, it was so quiet.

We got up from our seats, and Ben opened the door to the plane, lowering its self-contained stairs in the process. Jennifer appeared, running across the tarmac, screaming her joy at seeing us both again as we descended. My surprise showed, no doubt because my mouth was a gaping void. This was unexpected.

I looked at Ben, and he said tersely, "Jennifer brought the things I needed to pick up family stuff."

We hugged and kissed. Brad sauntered towards us too at a more sedate pace than his wife, accompanied by another couple. Lots of introductions were made of the new couple, Doug and Beth Wittman. Both were in their early thirties. Doug possessed an athletic body and had a deep tan suggesting he spent some time outside. Beth had short brunette hair and a shapely figure. She had what I call a 'bubble ass' making that part of her anatomy one of her outstanding features and a head-turner. I hugged both of them too.

We walked to the terminal, then stood outside in the late afternoon sunshine as the jet got serviced on the ramp. After the fuel truck pulled away from the airplane, Ben went inside and settled his fuel bill. I asked Ben how much the fuel bill had been, and he told me about four thousand five hundred dollars; I think my mouth fell open again.

We chattered at each other, reflected on the wedding and how lovely the Villa in Puerto Vallarta had been. Brad told me that he, Jennifer, Beth, and Doug had stayed at the house a year earlier and had been able to recommend it to Marc and Tiffany.

I grinned and asked Jennifer in a whisper, "Did you make love on the beach? You know, join the Beach Club?"

She grinned at me and said, "Yes. All four of us." Then she whispered to me again, "We swapped several times down there. Isn't it wonderful?"

I nodded enthusiastically. I could tell Jennifer had about a thousand questions. I pulled her aside and said, "We all made love on the beach while the moon was coming up. I'll never forget the past twenty-four hours. I don't think we'll try the Mile-high Club on this flight." She laughed, and we hugged.

Next, I knew Ben started pulling me towards the airplane, and we were waving goodbye again. "We'll be back soon," he told everyone.

All too soon, we repeated the process of checklists, taxiing, takeoff, and climb to altitude. With over a mile head start, we were at our flight level sooner than when we took off at sea level. As we flew our flight plan route at 41,000 feet, Ben pointed out that sunset on the ground occurred significantly earlier than it did for us at our altitude. Where there were no clouds, I could see the shadows of the evening already lengthening on the ground.

Soon dusk reached even our altitude, and in only a few minutes, we were night flying. Ben pointed out the nightlights of the Seattle area, and then we started our descent. We'd had a strong tailwind at altitude, so we had picked up almost an hour on our flight time. As we descended, I thought I could see Seattle from hundreds of miles away, and it turned out I could. Flying in the cockpit was so different from being in the back of the bus.

Many miles out, I heard Seattle Approach Control clear my mind just kept thinking that I will no longer be his when I get off this plane. Whatever the airport was telling us, I wasn't listening much.

Ben's hands flew around the cockpit, and he gave me a running commentary again on what he was doing. He had me read several checklists to him as we descended. When things got quiet, he pointed out the airport to me amidst the sea of lights surrounding Seattle. The airport was hard to see until I noticed the flashing green and white beacon.

Ben set the aircraft down so gently that the transition from flight to the ground was unnoticeable. After we slowed, he pulled off the active runway and taxied back to our hanger. Two linemen and a 'tug' were there to greet us. One of them indicated where we should park the jet with a pair of lighted batons.

Ben seemed happy as he gathered our gear from the storage locker at the back of the plane. He hummed and practically jumped around, clicking his heels. His hotness level went up fifty points at that moment.

One of the linemen pulled Ben's Porsche up beside the plane and put our suitcases and other bags into the back of the car. There appeared to be just enough space for all our things, mainly my souvenirs.

Ben drove us into Seattle. As we sat in the car, he asked if I was hungry.

Chapter Fourteen

Chapter Fifteen

"Not only am I hungry, but I think my throat's been cut. Several cokes are not my idea of a full meal on a flight." I grinned at him, yet inside, I wondered if now, after our wonderful weekend, we'd just go back to being coffee buddies once in a while. I had a little moment when I choked up and couldn't talk. Will I fall apart after this weekend?

"Good," Ben said, oblivious to my thoughts and emotions. "I think we have just enough time to make dinner at one of my favorite spots. Since the weather is so nice and clear, I'm sure you'll like it."

Ben shot around some of the roundabouts and crossed over the River onto the river's Seattle side. Next, I knew he took an exit and headed into the parking garage under Seattle's Center.

We locked up the car and went into the Collections café, a place I have never been but always wanted to. Collections Café is a one-of-a-kind space, offering a rare glimpse into Dale Chihuly's personal collections and design aesthetic. A life-long collector, Chihuly is often drawn to objects dating from the post-WWII era, many of which serve a particular function or appeal to his interests in form and color.

A hostess led us to a window table in the lounge, and we sat. Ben ordered us both a glass of wine. "Finally, I can have a drink," he said.

"Oh, that's right. Except for one glass of wine at the wedding, I haven't seen you drink anything alcoholic since we left."

Ben explained, "It has to do with being as sharp-witted as I can be as a pilot. The general rule is eight hours from bottle to throttle, but I try to be more conservative. Sometimes I'll not drink if I even think I might fly the next day. I enjoy wine, but I'm really not much of a drinker anyway."

We chatted some more and ordered a light dinner. A jazz trio was entertaining, the crowd was thin, and I attributed that to it being a Monday night. Ben and I were about the last to order. I blanched at the prices posted on the menu, but they didn't seem to bother Ben.

After a silence, I realized I was mildly jet-lagged and that the whirlwind weekend had started to catch up with me. Ben, on the other hand, had begun to come alive. He swept me up onto the dance floor.

"You know I like dancing with you," he told me. "I think we dance well together."

"Women like to dance," I said. "It's a sure way to a woman's heart."

"Vertical sex," Ben whispered in my ear. I ran my left hand up the back of his neck and into his hair. I leaned up and kissed his cheek.

"Thank you," he said. "You are genuine, aren't you?" We stopped dancing and walked the few paces back to our table.

"What you see is what you get," I said as we sat. "My mother always said if you try to be someone you aren't, the only person you'll end up fooling is yourself. I'd past twenty before I started to understand what she meant. People have to take me for who I am. I can accommodate, but I can't change."

"I like that philosophy," he said. After a long pause during which we stared out the windows, Ben suddenly asked me, "So did you like being my 'temporary girlfriend' for the weekend?"

I reached across the table and touched his hand. "It's changed my life forever. I can't say enough."

I paused and looked at him. My eyes started to tear up, and I got a knot in my throat suddenly. I couldn't talk through my tears. The realization that all this was going to end here and now. I didn't want this to end, and I had the sudden feeling that this was a 'thank you and goodbye' conversation. I'm going to be in my bedroom like Anna on *Fifty Shades* crying every night because Ben's out of my life. I didn't understand before why she was so upset about leaving him, but now I know. Anna loved him.

I choked and snorted a little as I held back a sob. "I'm sorry," I mumbled almost under my breath, "I just didn't want our time together to end."

Now Ben reached across the table and took my hand. "Neither do I."

"You don't?" I asked hope in my heart.

"Avery, you accept my family and my sister's lifestyle," Ben said. "As a child, my parents were the same way. I remember my parents having people stay at the house, and when I was old enough, I started to ask questions. Jennifer's kids have no clue what's going on because they don't do things with the kids around."

"Your parents were in the lifestyle," I stated, stunned by what he said.

"My sisters are my half-sisters. When Victor was born, a man came to the house, claiming that Victor was not my father's child. I thought it was crazy. My Mom and Dad were happily married. They had a DNA test done, and Victor was not my father's, but that didn't matter to him. He was on the birth certificate, and he didn't care. My dad ended up paying him off, and that was that I never saw him again. After that, my father had all of us tested. I didn't understand why, but he did. Come to find out that I'm his only child. I found out my Dad was in a car accident right after I was born, and he couldn't have kids. But he didn't know that before. Many of the people in the group were having sex. Also did the DNA test on the kids too. My father had two other children that he knew but was not raising. Let's go back to Victor. This man wanted my mother to leave us behind and marry him and bring Victor with her. My mom stayed with my father because they loved each other, and it didn't matter if the kids were my dad's DNA or not. They were his kids," Ben talking really fast. "This lifestyle is not easy, but it's all I know."

"I understand open relationships are real and out there, and I would rather be in a relationship like this than a BDSM one like *Fifty Shades*. I've had a threesome before, and I enjoyed it. I know you have too. What are you asking me?"

He slid from his chair and into the empty aisle of the lounge. Ben shuffled on his knees so he could be next to me, never once letting go of my hand.

Ben brought my hand to his lips and kissed it. "Avery ... will you marry me?"

I couldn't believe my ears. I broke into nearly uncontrollable crying as I screamed, "YES, YES, YES! Oh, I will, I will."

In my head, I was thinking, what did I just agree to. I had never been asked before, and I was excited. We will need a long engagement. I threw my arms around Ben, and we hugged and kissed. I couldn't believe I'd gone from near depression to elated joy in ten seconds.

Ben reached in his pocket and pulled out a diamond ring. The two or three-carat diamond was surrounded by a delicate pattern of baguettes and an antique hand-made setting. I'd never seen a ring like it.

He took my hand, and as about a hundred patrons and staff watched us, he slipped the ring on my finger. I then leaped out of my chair and into his arms.

"Oh, Ben. I'm so glad ... happy ... everything." I was all teary again. I sobbed, almost uncontrollably for a minute.

Other patrons watched, and it didn't take too much imagination to figure out what had just happened between the two of us. We both sat down again. Ben would have kept holding both of my hands, but I had to wipe the tears of joy from my eyes frequently to see. Eventually, I looked around the lounge; many smiling faces and heads were nodding in our direction.

Then suddenly, our waitress, the hostess, and the bartender all came over carrying a cupcake with a sparkler going full tilt on it. Our waitress said, "You two just made everyone here feel good. Congratulations from all of us." Everyone, even the other patrons - applauded. Now I was blushing. We thanked everyone.

I was speechless, a rare state for me. My brain had a thousand questions to ask. All I could do is be silent, wipe my teary eyes. I maintained my silly smile of ultimate happiness and kept looking at the ring on my left hand. It could have been plastic, but instead, it was this beautiful piece of art. Ben seemed pretty happy too, and pleased with himself.

Ben explained, "The ring belonged to my mother's mother. It's a family heirloom."

"OH," I exclaimed as I suddenly connected the dots. "Is this why we stopped in Denver?"

"Yeah," he said in a humble voice. "Jennifer had been keeping the ring in Denver for my eventual use. She and Tiffany had a bet that I'd never claim it or give it to anyone." I stammered, "So ... so you knew in Mexico? Before we left? Did Tiffany and Melissa know?"

"I actually knew in Aspen before we went to Mexico, and yes, Tiffany and Melissa knew. Jennifer had to get the ring from her safe deposit box this morning. Tiffany called her just after we left Puerto Vallarta to tell her when we were arriving in Denver and to tell her not to spill the beans. Avery, you are so perfect. You are every guy's best dream, and I don't want to have you anywhere other than in my life all the time, forever and ever."

"Last Thursday at dinner and on our flight, I told you my philosophy about relationships. I meant it. We're going to have an open marriage. I want us to be each other's home base, but I want us to keep growing, learning, and finding joy in the world for ourselves. I know other people will provide those avenues to you, and sometimes that will involve intimacy of some kind. I don't mind and hope you won't."

I paused and said, "When I go into work tomorrow, and my friends ask me how my weekend went. I will absolutely blow everyone's mind telling them I got engaged to a guy I met a week ago. My parents are going to be blown away too." "Regrets?" Ben asked with a twinkle in his eye.

"Not one iota," I said with a big grin. "Wait, we haven't been with a third person, or well, we had someone watching us have sex. I knew someone was watching, and I didn't care. We have not had a third person in our bed together and saw how we act?" I leaned across the table and kissed Ben again.

"I talked to Melissa before we left about being our third to see if it would work," Ben said.

"What did she say?" I asked.

"Melissa's all for it. After the honeymoon, she has business in Seattle, so she is coming, down to have a threesome to see if we can handle it," Ben said.

"What if I can't handle you with someone else?" I asked.

"Well, then we will find interesting ways to make our love life great with just the two of us," Ben said. I reached over and hugged him tightly. Ben stood. "Let's go home."

We swung by my apartment and picked up a few more clothes that I held on my lap as we drove to Ben's condo. I moved in that night at his insistence. Over the following weeks, I gradually created Avery spaces that had been exclusively Ben spaces. He didn't mind a bit and helped me every step of the way.

Chapter Sixteen

We went and picked up Melissa a month after the wedding. I had moved in, and Ben paid for my apartment for the last three months. I wouldn't be in trouble for breaking the leases. I feel like I'm jumping into the big pool with all this, but it was time to find out. We went out to dinner with Melissa and just got home, and everything was really awkward. I realized someone had to start. None of us were drunk. We each a glass of wine, so you can't blame it on that. I looked at Ben, took Ben's hand in mine, and then reached for Melissa's hand. "Come and join us for the night." I made the invitation in a soft and loving tone of voice so there would be no mistaking the warmth and affection I felt for both of them.

Ben moved forward and pulled the two of us into a group hug with him. It seemed so natural, and we flowed up the stairs and into our bedroom.

I lit a candle, and by that single light, we gradually disrobed each other. When we were nude, Melissa and I pushed Ben onto his back on the bed. Soon the two of us were having fun playing with Ben's hardening rod as he watched us and stroked the parts of us he could reach. He groaned a lot.

Finally, he said, "One of you, come up and kiss me and let me lick you."

I gestured to Melissa, "Go. We both want to taste you tonight. He's first."

Melissa moved up and kissed Ben as he fondled her breasts. Then she moved further up the bed and straddled Ben's head as she held the headboard. I watched as she lowered her pussy into his face. I could see his tongue reaching far out of his mouth as he started to savor her juices.

I messaged Ben's cock and then straddled his legs until I could lower my pussy onto his lovemaking tool. Every nerve in my body became alive as I slipped myself down onto his shaft. My juices flowed excessively, even running down my leg as I moved ever so slowly up and down, enjoying every penetrating fraction of an inch of his large cock.

I moved up and down on Ben's cock, enjoying the sensations and the connection with him. Further, it was so erotic watching him lick and tongue Melissa's pussy. I smoothed her body as I ground my pussy into Ben's loins.

"I'm going to cum," I soon announced to my partners.

I closed my eyes and let the orgasm sweep up my body from where I'd made his cock rub against my clitoris. My breathing ceased for a few seconds. My eyes were closed, yet I watched the most extraordinary exhibition of fireworks and lasers flashing across the sky. If I wasn't in love with these people before, I was now.

When I opened my eyes again, Melissa was right there kissing me, one hand still lightly stroking my clit. Had she brought me off? I couldn't tell you what had happened for the past couple of minutes.

She smiled at me. "I like how you cum. You let me bring you off. That's good. Trusting." She kissed me again. I vaguely remembered now, just as I started my ascent to the stars, an extra hand massaging my nub.

I suddenly felt a twitch from Ben deep within me. I turned to him; "Did you cum?"

"No," he smiled as he stroked my sides with both hands.

I rolled off of him to one side. "Then make love to Melissa."

He nodded, and I positioned Melissa next to him. She spread her legs, expecting Ben to mount her. However, instead, I leaned forward before Ben could place himself and took a long lap up her pussy.

I returned immediately, pulled her labia lips into my own, and then flicked my tongue across her clit. I could feel her twitch as I hit pay dirt. With one hand, I gently thrust two fingers into her pussy and searched for her G-spot. I became certain I'd found the area when Melissa's hips leaped off the bed, and she emitted a long, low moan.

Ben joined me side by side, and we took turns lapping and stimulating Melissa. Each of us had a hand on one of her breasts, massaging and pinching as her nipples reached an excellent state of excitement.

Then Melissa came. She erupted. I'd seen a porn film one time where a girl came in buckets and almost covered everyone in the room. Melissa wasn't that prolific, but she did squirt into our faces and onto our bodies as she came. She also screamed, so I was sure everyone else in the house knew what we were doing.

"Fuck her, Ben," I said quietly. "Do it now. Make her cum again."

Ben rose, and I took his steel rod in my hand and guided it to Melissa's sopping pussy. I rubbed the head around and then urged Ben to push at just the right place. I had a closeup view as his long shaft slowly sank to the hilt in her pussy. They both groaned, and to tell the truth, I did too as I felt a surge of juice in my own pussy, a sympathetic response.

Ben established slow and deliberate stroking in and out of Melissa's body. They both smiled and kissed, pulling me into the fray as they did.

"Bring your pussy up over my mouth, Avery," Melissa instructed.

I rose and positioned myself facing Ben but in a way that Melissa could tongue my slit and nether region. I held Ben's shoulders for stability and also to feel more a part of his thrusting into Melissa. Ben and I could kiss, and we did; he fondled my breasts with one hand, using the other to steady us and to fondle Melissa's generous breasts.

Except from Christmas With Avery

Melissa's tongue proved to be expert, for in no time at all, I found myself writhing above her and nearing orgasm again.

"I'm getting near again," I warned my partners.

"Me too," Ben said softly.

"Me too," Melissa whispered.

Thirty seconds later, Ben sped up his thrusts into Melissa as she accelerated her tongue action on my cunt. One of her fingers jamming me at a rapid rate. I reached down and massaged her clit, trying to deliver exceptional stimulation to the small area.

We exploded.

Ben led the way by making several final deep penetrations. He shot his cum into Melissa; Melissa and my orgasms followed directly. We all got wet again, and I think I was the culprit this time. We both cuddled into Ben in our afterglow, enjoying the aromas we'd created and the stickiness we shared. No one wanted to do anything about it.

No one said a word. We could feel each other's hearts beating and listen to the softening sounds of our breathing. One by one by one, we closed our eyes and fell asleep in each other's arms. I'm not sure I'd ever felt so content in my life. *Read the next book in the series Christmas With Avery*

About the Author

Tammy Godfrey has called Southeast Idaho home for the vast majority of her life. She survived sixteen years in the military, and she is proud of almost every minute of it. After leaving the camouflage uniform behind she decided she needed to do something productive with the time tat she wasn't taking care of her husband and kids. When she wasn't lost in the exciting world of tax preparation, she was hitting the books at Idaho State University seeking a degree in something practical like business. During her time in the world of academia she discovered a love for writing. After spending long days and nights overcoming her fear of the blank page her first book was published in 2013. She is currently working hard on her next novel. Tammy loves everything geek, including her adorable husband, and loves working on crafty things, reading, and going to comic con. Tammy believes that Murphy's Law has played a large part in her life. If anything weird can happen, it will. One
  thing that can be said about Tammy Godfrey, she's not boring.

Also by Tammy Godfrey

Murder on the Morning Mist

Natalie Hart was a divorced mother of four. The four kids have grown and left the small town of Bear Lake, the ex-husband has not. Having her ex, and the woman he cheated on her with, living in the same town was just one of several issues that plaque Nat's thoughts every morning when she goes out on a run. There's the family Inn that she tries to manage, and a family curse that she tries to forget. Nat began her typical day with a typical run, expecting to find what she always found, a brisk mountain breeze, squirrels in the trees, and the stillness of the calm lake. It's the lake that brings the tourists, and they bring the money that keeps the town going. But the one thing Natalie Hart didn't expect to find could change the town forever. It will bring danger and mystery, bad boys from the recent past, and treasures from long past. It will reveal secrets, and those who want the secrets kept. You should be careful when you go for a run in the morning mist, you never know what you're going to find, and you may never stop running.